ALIEN ESCAPE!

GUY BASS

ILLUSTRATED BY FRED BLUNT

TO MY LITTLE SISTER, LIZZIE

First published in the UK in 2010 by Scholastic Children's Books
An imprint of Scholastic Ltd
Euston House, 24 Eversholt Street
London, NW1 1DB, UK
Registered office: Westfield Road, Southam, Warwickshire, CV47 0RA
SCHOLASTIC and associated logos are trademarks and/or registered trademarks
of Scholastic Inc.

Text copyright © Guy Bass, 2010
Illustrations copyright © Fred Blunt, 2010

The right of Guy Bass and Fred Blunt to be identified as the author
and illustrator of this work has been asserted by them.

Cover illustration © Fred Blunt, 2010

ISBN 978 1 407 11122 3

A CIP catalogue record for this book is available
from the British Library.

Printed by CPI Bookmarque, Croydon, CR0 4TD
Papers used by Scholastic Children's Books are made from
wood grown in sustainable forests.

1 3 5 7 9 10 8 6 4 2

www.scholastic.co.uk/zone
www.guybass.com

THIS BOOK BELONGS TO:

Her Majestic Green,
the Empress Valoona XIII

(ALONG WITH EVERYTHING
ELSE ON **PLANET X**)

DAMAGE TO THIS BOOK, INCLUDING TEARS,
GLOOP-STAINS AND RAY-GUN SCORCHING, WHETHER DELIBERATE
OR ACCIDENTAL, WILL RESULT IN DISINTEGRATION

DISINTEGRATE FOR VICTORY!

JOIN THE INVASION EFFORT AND HELP
DISINTEGRATE THE ENEMIES OF PLANET X!

(ANYONE NOT JOINING THE EFFORT WILL BE DISINTEGRATED.)

THE GREAT GREEN HALL

The Great Green Hall was filled to bursting. Hex had never seen so many planetexians in one place before! But why were they all there? And, more importantly, what was *he* doing there?

"Move!" said a voice behind him. Hex looked back to see two planetexian guards, dressed in impressive silver and green uniforms. Without warning, one of them jabbed him in the back with an electric prod-rod.

"Yow!" said Hex, stumbling forward. His eyes darted nervously around the gathered planetexians. There, in the crowd, was his mother, looking very disappointed. Soon, Hex spotted more familiar faces – his friends from school, Dooper and Opo, and even Opo's unbearable brother, Steek, looking thoroughly smug.

Hex tried desperately to remember how he'd got into this mess. A moment later, he caught sight of a fat planetexian at the end of the hall. She was sitting on a grand, floating throne, with an ornate crown pushed tightly over her enormous brain-sack.

It was the empress.

"Her Majestic Green, the Empress Valoona XIII!" came a cry. At once, the crowd fell to their knees and bowed deeply. Everyone except Hex. He was frozen to the spot, unable to move, as the empress floated towards him on her gravity-defying throne. Hex held his gill-breath as the empress's third eye opened and inspected him closely.

"Hex-37," she snarled, her telepathy nodes pulsing. "We meet at last."

"Uh, hi," whimpered Hex, meekly waving a sucker.

"You have been accused of the most un-green treachery," hissed the empress. "You have betrayed your people, you have betrayed your planet, and you have betrayed your family and friends! But worst of all, you have betrayed . . . me!"

"No, please, it's not like that. I just wanted to help my dad!" Hex cried. "It's all the Hex Effect's fault!"

"This is my planet – mine!" snarled the empress. "All I've ever asked from you is a little space invading. Is that too much to expect? You are a planetexian, aren't you? And what do planetexians love?"

"SPACE INVADING!" shouted the crowd.

"Exactly! But not you – oh no, *you* had to be different!" barked the empress. "Well different won't do, not on my planet! For we all know that difference leads to. . ."

"DISINTEGRATION!" yelled the gathered planetexians.

The empress pointed a sucker into the air, and Hex looked up to see three huge sentry-bots float down from the ceiling. Hex screamed, but he was drowned out by chants of "DISINTEGRATE! DISINTEGRATE!".

The empress smiled. "Goodbye, Hex," she said, "and good morning!"

Good morning? thought Hex, as the sentry-bots took aim.

ZWAAARK!

"NooOOOoo!" screamed Hex, sitting bolt upright and bashing his antenna on the top of his slumber pod. It was a dream! Hex rubbed his eyes and checked that he had all his suckers and gills, nervous green sweat running down his forehead.

☆ ☆
☆ 4 ☆

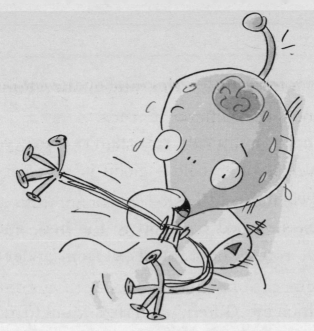

"I *said*, good morning!" said T.K.421, the computer that operated Hex's hover-home in the skies just outside New X City. A robotic pincer snaked out of the wall and pulled off Hex's sheet. "Time to get up! It's another beautiful day on Planet X! The suns are shining, radiation levels are just above tolerable and there's only a 26.6 per cent chance of acid rain! So, are you looking forward to another day of space invader training?"

"Can't wait. Look, would you give me a few minutes, T.K.?" said Hex, as the robotic pincer tried to lift Hex out of the slumber pod by his ankle.

"Three minutes! You don't want your breakfast to go cold – gloop is best served lukewarm!" said T.K.

Hex slumped back on to the bed, and a small, round robot rolled out from under his pillow.

"Pinch me, Glitch," said Hex. "Just to make sure I'm not still dreaming."

Hex's friend (and his best invention to date) stared at his green-skinned companion in confusion. "Click-POP?" Glitch asked.

"Of course I'm serious," said Hex.

Glitch shrugged, reached out a tiny robotic arm and pinched Hex on the sucker.

"Ow! Thanks," said Hex. "I needed that."

"Kik-kik-POP-POP?" asked Glitch.

"Yeah, another nightmare, the same as all the others," sighed Hex. "It's like I'm on trial or something, for tricking the empress into calling off the invasion of Earth. And then just as I'm about to get disintegrated, I wake up."

Only a week ago, Hex-37 had single-suckeredly prevented the invasion of a muddy little planet called Earth. It wasn't that he particularly cared about saving the earthlings – after all, he was used to Planet X conquering world after world. It was all planetexians ever did, or seemed to think about. But Hex had found out that his *father* was on Earth, and that had changed everything.

Hex had always thought his dad had been lost in space during a routine hypersaucer lesson, but in truth (and by sheer bad luck), his dad had ended up on the same world that Planet X was preparing to invade. Hex knew then that he had to try and save his father, but he had no idea how.

Hex still couldn't understand how he'd succeeded – how he'd found himself disguised as an earthling, or how he'd teleported to the royal palace and scared the empress into cancelling the invasion. There was only one explanation for all the strange things that had happened – a family curse known as the "Hex Effect".

Whether it was good luck or bad, from the moment Hex had started space invader training, the Hex Effect had changed his life for ever. Despite being years ahead of his classmates when it came to technology and robotics, Hex had the worst luck with anything to do with space invading. Ray-guns, hypersaucers – you name it. They would all suddenly malfunction. It had been the same for Hex's dad, and his dad before him, and so on, for thirty-six generations – as soon as the Hexes started space invader training, anything that could go wrong, did go wrong.

PING! PING!

Hex reached over to his bedside table

and picked up his Personal Advice Device. "Dad?" he said.

Hex waited a moment, staring at the small, silver object resting in his sucker. Not only did his P.A.D. contain a constantly updated database of *Everything you need to know about Space Invading, but were afraid to ask*, but it was the only way his father could contact him from Earth.

MORNING, SON. DID YOU SLEEP WELL?

"I'm still not completely sure I've woken up," replied Hex, rubbing his huge, oval eyes.

ANOTHER NIGHTMARE?

"Half the time I can't sleep, and the rest of the time I have nightmares!" groaned Hex. "I just can't shake the feeling that someone's going to find out what I did."

EVERYTHING IS GOING TO BE OK, SON. THERE'S NO WAY THE EMPRESS COULD KNOW IT WAS YOU UNDERNEATH THAT EARTHLING DISGUISE.

"But how can you be sure? What if she's realized I wasn't a real earthling? What if she sends her guards to get me . . . or her sentry-bots?" said Hex, working himself into a green lather.

BUT SHE HASN'T, HEX. BELIEVE ME, IT'S GOING TO BE FINE. THE ONLY WAY ANYONE IS GOING TO FIND OUT WHAT YOU DID IS IF YOU ACTUALLY CONFESS, AND THERE'S NO WAY THAT'S NOT GOING TO HAPPEN, IS THERE?

"No way . . . I'm keeping my mouth and telepathy nodes shut. I haven't even told Mum," said Hex.

I THINK WE BOTH KNOW THAT'S FOR THE BEST. I THINK YOUR MOTHER'S THE <u>LAST</u> PERSON YOU SHOULD TELL

ABOUT YOUR LITTLE ADVENTURE. I CAN JUST IMAGINE HOW MUCH SHE WAS LOOKING FORWARD TO INVADING EARTH.

"Yeah, she was pretty excited," sighed Hex.

IN FACT, IT'S BEST THAT NO ONE - ESPECIALLY YOUR MUM - FINDS OUT ABOUT ME. YOU SHOULD MAKE SURE YOU DELETE MY MESSAGES FROM YOUR P.A.D. INBOX. YOU DON'T WANT ANYONE CHECKING IT WHILE YOU'RE NOT LOOKING.

"OK, Dad," said Hex, sadly. As great as it was to know that his dad was alive, it made Hex wish he could trust his mum with his secret. But Hex knew she put space invading before anything else. After all, everyone on Planet X did.

SO, HAVE YOU THOUGHT ANY MORE ABOUT COMING TO EARTH? THE SOONER YOU'RE AWAY FROM PLANET X, THE BETTER.

"Uh, I have to go, Dad . . . I'm late for school," said Hex. "I'll talk to you at lunchtime, OK?"

He turned off the P.A.D. quickly. It wasn't that he didn't want to escape to Earth – he would give anything to get off Planet X, especially now. Plus his dad made Earth sound very appealing, even if they did only have one sun. But Hex was so scared of being found out that the idea of trying to escape filled him with dread.

Hex was about to delete his Dad's messages from his P.A.D. when a robotic pincer grabbed him by the ankle and dragged him out of his slumber pod.

"Three minutes are up!" said T.K.421. "You've got a long and glorious day of space invading ahead of you!"

HEX'S PRESENT

Once washed, scrubbed and dressed in his silver uniform, complete with his unpredictable, ancient tele-belt (the Hex Effect had destroyed his first one), Hex slipped Glitch into his pocket and stepped on the conveyor belt. He was immediately whisked into the ingestion zone for breakfast.

"DIE, ALIEN SCUM!" cried his mother, pointing a ray-gun right in his face!

"Waaaaaaaah!" screamed Hex and dived on to the ground.

"Sorry, just practising ... honestly, Hex, you've been so jumpy lately," said his mother, spinning the ray-gun around her sucker. "I just wanted to show you your new present."

"Pr-present?" said Hex, nervously. Hex's mother held out her sucker and handed Hex the ray-gun.

"A ray-gun?" said Hex, staring worriedly at the red, oval-shaped pistol. Any other planetexian would have been pleased with such an impressive present, but the Hex

Effect had a way of making sure nothing worked as it was supposed to.

"I know it's not your hatching day for another month or so, but since the empress called off the attack on Planet Earth, I thought you could do with some fun!" she said. As captain of the 101st hypersaucer fleet, Hex's mother was one of the best space invaders on Planet X. Hex had never met anyone who loved space invading so much – the only time she was really happy was when she was blowing things up.

"Thanks, Mum," he said, forcing a smile as he clipped the ray-gun to his tele-belt. "It's . . . it's just what I wanted."

"Oh good, I hoped you'd like it," said his mother, putting a sucker on his shoulder. "You know what they say, a space invader without a ray-gun is like a nudlork without puss-ducts."

"Uh, did my replacement tele-belt arrive? I

still can't seem to fix this one," asked Hex. "I was teleported to the wrong training zone six times last week. I don't even have to turn it on any more – once it teleported me on to the school roof in the middle of a lesson! I mean it did get me out of crop circle training, but. . ."

"Sorry, Hex, you'll have to put up with it for a while. There's been a delay at the factory. All production has halted until the empress's new project is finished – some sort of new *super* sentry-bot," said his mum, turning on the news-vid.

"Following the recent attack on New X City by the pathetic, mud-sucking earthlings who aren't even worth invading anyway, Her Majestic Green, the Empress Valoona XIII, has ordered the construction of the *ultimate* planetary protector – a super sentry-bot, capable of repelling any invader and crushing any enemy!"

A picture of an enormous robot appeared on the vid-screen. It looked very much like the sentry-bots Hex had encountered on his "accidental" trip to the empress's palace, with a massive, bucket-shaped body, immense shoulder-mounted ray-cannons and sharp, metal pincers. But this robot was *huge*, at least three times bigger than a hypersaucer! It was easily the most impressive thing Hex had ever seen and made his own robotic creations pale in comparison.

"Amazing," he whispered.

"Klik-ka-chik-kik!" huffed Glitch, jealously, from Hex's pocket.

"Sorry, Glitch. You know you're still my number one bot," whispered Hex.

"What?" asked his mother.

"I said, uh, it looks like it couldn't be stopped!" replied Hex, pushing Glitch back in his pocket. Hex knew how much his mum hated his robot-making hobby, and did his best to keep Glitch hidden.

"It certainly does. How generous of the empress to provide us with a global guardian – no one will dare attack us again!" said Hex's mum.

Hex bit his lip. He could never tell his mum that he was the one who had "attacked" New X City in a hypersaucer – yet another accident caused by the Hex Effect.

"Two minutes till the skybus arrives! Eat up, Hex!" said T.K., placing two bowls of gloop on the table. Hex scrunched his face up. Gloop was the only food on Planet X and Hex hated it at the best of times. Today, with a belly full of nerves, he began to feel more than a little queasy. He pushed the gloop bowl aside and made his way to the ejection chute. As he was launched on to the waiting platform, he took out his P.A.D. again, and turned it on. He leant into the P.A.D. and whispered, "I want to get away."

There was a pause.

IT SOUNDS LIKE YOU WANT TO ESCAPE FROM PLANET X. IS THIS TRUE? IF SO, PLEASE SAY YES . . .

. . . AND THE PLANETEXIAN POLICE WILL BE WITH YOU IN A FEW MOMENTS TO ARREST YOU AND TAKE YOU DIRECTLY TO YOUR NEAREST DISINTEGRATION CHAMBER.

IF THIS IS NOT TRUE, PLEASE SAY NO.

"No! No, it's not true! I don't want to escape! Everything's fine!" shrieked Hex and quickly turned off his P.A.D. That settled it. There was no way he was trying to escape – it was just too risky. Before long, the skybus appeared in the distance, snaking across the pink planetexian sky. Hex sloped on, hoping that he could make it through one day at Sporg's School for Space Invaders without anything bad happening.

"BOOM!"

MIND-CONTROL TRAINING

At the sound of the **"BOOM!"** Hex let out a panicked yelp and threw himself to the floor of the skybus ... but then immediately realized it was just his friend, Dooper (the biggest boy in his class by a good antenna's length), getting excited about blowing things up. The other children (and even the skybus driver) started laughing at Hex, and didn't stop till he shuffled into the seat next to Dooper.

"Hey, Hex! I was just telling everyone about my trip to the Disintegration Range this weekend. I disintegrated fifty-eight target-bots – in thirty-nine seconds! It was a new record! BOOM! **BOOM!**" he bellowed, blowing the end of his suckers as if they were ray-gun barrels.

"Uh, is there any way we could not talk about disintegration, just for today?" asked Hex.

"Are you OK, Hex?" said Opo, leaning over the seat in front of him. "You look like you haven't slept in a week."

"I wish I hadn't," said Hex, rubbing his tired eyes and attempting a smile.

If anyone might understand about his predicament, it would be Opo. She was the only other creature on Planet X who knew that it was Hex who had accidentally attacked New X City during hypersaucer training, and she hadn't told anyone about it.

But what if she found out he had deliberately made the empress call off the invasion of Earth? Even if she wasn't the biggest fan of space invading, would she really betray the empress? Hex couldn't risk trusting her – or anyone else. As far as he was concerned, honesty could only lead to one thing – disintegration.

"What's the matter, Hex-37? Is the training too much for you?" sneered Steek from across the aisle. Opo's twin brother was the one planetexian (apart from the empress) that Hex would be happy never to see again.

"Face facts," Steek continued, "you Hexes just aren't cut out for space invading."

"Shut your gills, *Stink*! Team Dooper and Hex will be blowing stuff up before you even finish your first year!" bellowed Dooper.

"I wasn't talking to you, *Dopey*. Why don't you keep your antenna out of my face, you big, fat bowl of gloop," snarled Steek.

"I've already told you, I'm not fat! I have overactive elbow glands!" protested Dooper.

"Ignore him, Hex," said Opo. "The thing

you have to remember about my brother is he doesn't know how to be anything other than a pain in the nodes. . ."

"Hey, is that a ray-gun?" said Steek, spotting Hex's present clipped to his tele-belt. "Who on Planet X thought it was a good idea to give *you* a ray-gun?"

"My, uh, my mum bought it for me," replied Hex, quietly.

"What was she thinking?" said Steek. "Doesn't she know about the Hex Effect? You're the last person on Planet X who should have a ray-gun! Knowing you, you'll end up disintegrating someone . . . or yourself!"

Steek continued to prod and pester Hex about being disintegrated all the way to Sporg's School for Space Invaders. By the time they arrived, Hex's nerves were more shredded than ever.

The children herded into the school, and then Hex and the rest of Roswell class teleported to training zone 13, where their teacher, Miss Voob, was waiting for them.

As Hex materialized in the training zone, he was grateful that at least his tele-belt seemed to be working today. For a moment, Hex wondered if the Hex Effect had actually worn off.

"Pay attention, Roswell class," said Miss Voob. "Today we are going to be learning about mind-control, a vital tool in any invader's arsenal."

The class saw the blue glow of teleportation energy appear in the middle of the zone. A second later, a green box appeared on Miss Voob's desk. She opened it and took out a silver, bowl-shaped contraption. "This is a *minding module*," she continued. "It will allow you to read thoughts, befuddle your enemies, and even command them to do your—"

"MISS VOOB, REPORT IMMEDIATELY TO TRAINING ZONE 51. CLASS SUPERVISION

REQUIRED IN TRAINING ZONE 51," said a voice over the tannoy.

"Oh, for goodness' sake . . . where are the assisto-bots when you need them?" moaned Miss Voob. "Honestly, it's all very well the school's bots helping to build the empress's new super sentry-bot, but I'm left running around like a blue-bottomed beezle! Right, I'll be five minutes – who can I trust with the minding module until then?"

"Pick me! Pick me!" cried Steek. "I'm responsible!"

"Ah, Steek – eager as ever," smiled Miss Voob as she handed Steek the minding module. "In the meantime, everyone take out your P.A.D.s and find out all you can about how to use the minding module."

As Miss Voob de-materialized and Steek proudly cradled the minding module, everyone unclipped their P.A.D.s from their belts and turned them on. Hex sighed and mumbled "minding module" into his P.A.D.

PING!

IT LOOKS LIKE YOU ARE TRYING TO BE
TELEPATHIC. CAN I HELP?

"Telepathic?" whispered Hex, nervous of
what was coming next.

INVADING CAN BE A TRICKY BUSINESS.
YOU MIGHT FIND YOURSELF ON A STRANGE
PLANET, FULL OF CREATURES THAT DO NOT
SPEAK YOUR LANGUAGE, AND WHO ARE NOT
TOO KEEN ON BEING INVADED. NO PROBLEM!
WITH THE MINDING MODULE YOU CAN FIND
OUT EVERYTHING YOU NEED TO KNOW FROM
THEM, AND GET THEM TO DO WHAT YOU WANT,
WITHOUT EVEN RAISING A SUCKER. WHY
DISINTEGRATE YOUR ENEMY, WHEN YOU CAN
GET THEM TO DISINTEGRATE THEMSELVES?
HERE IS HOW IT WORKS:

ATTACH THE MINDING MODULE TO YOUR
TELEPATHY NODES

CHOOSE FROM ONE OF THE TWO SETTINGS:
CONTROL — ALLOWS YOU TO CONTROL YOUR
VICTIM'S EVERY MOVE!

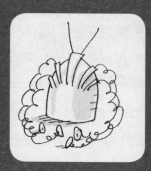

"*Mind-reading?*" whispered Hex, frantically. "I can't have my mind read!"

"Chik! POP!" said Glitch in agreement, poking his head out of Hex's pocket.

"Right, let's get started," said Steek, fixing the minding module to his telepathy nodes.

"I don't think we should be messing around with that thing," said Hex, nervously. "What if something went wrong?"

"I couldn't agree more . . . which is exactly why only *I* will be using it," said Steek, and turned the dial to CONTROL.

"Don't worry, Hex – Stink couldn't control

a nudlork, and they don't even *have* brains!" whispered Dooper to Hex, but Dooper's whispers were always loud enough for the whole class to hear.

"You fat gwirm, you can't talk about me like that!" snarled Steek, pointing the minding module at Dooper.

"Hey, my head feels fuzzy, no, fizzy, no, squelchy. . ." said Dooper, grabbing his brain-sack. "What's going –" began Dooper, and then suddenly froze.

"Dooper, are you OK?" asked Hex. Dooper stood still for a moment and then turned to Hex – a strange, blank look in his eyes.

"I am a fat gwirm. I smell like a scum-bug and I live in the spit-pools of swamp gulpers, because I am stupider than a skeeble's armpit and twice as ugly," said Dooper, his eyes glazed. "Oh, and I *don't* have overactive elbow glands, I just like to stuff my face with gloop! I'm a stupid fat gloop-head!"

Dooper started waving his arms about like a hungry gwirm and jumping up and down. Steek was controlling him! The other children started laughing as Dooper hopped around the zone on one foot, shouting, "Gloop-head! Gloop-head! I'm a stupid gloop-head!"

"Look at him go!" laughed Steek.

"Knock it off, Steek!" shouted Hex.

"Hex is right, Steek – that's enough!" said Opo.

"Sorry, Hex, but Miss Voob left *me* in charge, not you," grinned Steek, making Dooper run face first into a wall!

"Leave him alone!" said Hex, trying to grab the minding module off Steek's head.

"Get off me! You don't know who you're messing with. . ." said Steek, and Hex suddenly felt huge suckers grab him by the shoulders and lift him into the air. It was Dooper, still firmly under Steek's control.

"You're a super stupid gloop-head too, Hex!" said Dooper, clutching Hex in a vice-like grip. "Team Dooper and Hex, the super stupid gloop-head team. Let's do the stupid gloop-head team dance!"

Dooper started dancing Hex around the zone! He spun him around by his suckers, lifting him into the air!

"S-stop, Dooper – I mean Steek!" cried Hex.

"POP! POP!" said Glitch, falling out of Hex's pocket.

"Ha! Don't they make a lovely couple? Dance, you gloop-heads, dance!" laughed Steek. Then he noticed the ray-gun on Hex's tele-belt. He grinned and commanded Dooper to grab it. Dooper let go of Hex, who went flying into a wall! Hex rubbed his sore brain-sack and then looked up. Dooper was pointing the ray-gun right at him.

"It'd be so easy to put you out of your

misery," whispered Steek. "You never know, I might get a medal for services to the empress. . ."

"You . . . you wouldn't!" said Hex.

"Wouldn't I?" hissed Steek.

KRUMP!

Opo leapt on Steek, pushing him face first into the ground! She tried to pull the minding module off his head, but he was wriggling too much for her to grab hold of it. Finally, she managed to turn the minding module dial from CONTROL to PROBE.

"There," she said, pinning him to the ground. "You should be controlling yourself, not anyone else. Now behave, or I'll feed you your magna-boots again!"

"Get off me!" screamed Steek. "I'm in charge! You're breaking school rules!"

"What. . . what happened?" said a confused Dooper. "My brain feels floppy, no, squishy, no, crunchy. . ." A moment later he looked down at his suckers. "Hey, cool, I've got a ray-gun! BOOM!"

"Maybe you should keep it, it suits you more than me, anyway," said Hex, as he felt a little dizzy himself.

"What the – what's going on?" muttered Hex, grabbing his head. After a moment, he spotted Steek, glaring at him. Hex slowly realized what was happening – Steek was trying to read his mind! It felt as if his thoughts were being sucked out of his brain! And they were all secret thoughts!

Disintegration! Hypersaucers! Mindless violence! thought Hex, trying to fill his head with space invader related thoughts, but they just reminded him of his secrets!

"It's working!" cried Steek, finally managing to throw Opo off him. He got to his feet and began striding towards Hex. "I'm reading his mind! I'm . . . wait a minute, what – YOW-OW-oW!"

Suddenly Steek was hopping from foot to foot, trying to prise the module from his head as sparks and smoke filled the air! "Get it off! Get it off!"

The gathered children tried to stifle their giggles. Finally, Steek managed to tear the minding module off his head and threw it to the ground. A few good stamps later and it was lying in pieces.

Hex couldn't believe it. Could it have been the Hex Effect? It had never worked in his favour before – at least not directly. For a moment, Hex wondered if things were looking up.

But only for a moment.

"What in the name of the empress's emerald underwear is going on here?" said Miss Voob, re-materializing in the training zone. "Steek, are you all right? Why is there smoke coming off your brain-sack?"

"Dad . . . alive . . . Dad. . ." Steek said,

clutching his head. Hex froze in horror.

"'Dad? Whose dad? You're not making any sense, Steek," said Miss Voob.

"I read his mind!" cried Steek. "Hex's dad is alive . . . on Earth!"

SECRETS AND LIES
(AND SPACE INVASION)

"No, no, no," said Miss Voob, as Roswell class gathered around. "I'm afraid Hex's dad isn't the least bit alive – he was sucked into a black hole. Isn't that right, Hex?"

"What? Oh yes! Absolutely!" agreed Hex, quickly.

"It's not true! I mean, yes, he was sucked into a black – look, that's not the point!" cried Steek. "I saw it in my head, just before the minding module blew up! Hex is lying! His dad's alive and well . . . and living on that stinking mudball, Earth!"

"Earth? *Planet* Earth? What are you talking about? Hex, did Steek read your mind? Is any of this true?" asked Miss Voob, firmly.

Hex panicked. This was it – he'd been found out! He looked around for an escape route, but there was nowhere to run. He reached down to his tele-belt. Maybe if he turned it on it would pick up some random signal and teleport him to the other side of Planet X!

"Excuse me, Miss Voob, but it's my brother who's lying," said Opo. "Steek would do *anything* to get Hex into trouble."

"Yeah, Stink hates Hex!" bellowed Dooper. "He treats him like a glob of gloop on his magna-boot!"

"What? I'm not lying! It's that mucus-spewing slurm-slug who's lying! I read his mind! And there's more . . . I just can't – I just can't get it straight in my head," said Steek, rubbing his telepathy nodes.

"You're such a greeny-meanie!" said Opo, firmly. "Of *course* Hex wishes his dad was still alive. Don't you wish the same about Mum?"

"What? Well yes, but it's not a wish, it's—" began Steek.

"So maybe if you could stop being such a mean old gwirm for two seconds, you'd see how bad it makes Hex feel," said Opo, prodding Steek with a sucker.

"No, that's not the point! Hex is—" tried Steek, but Miss Voob put a sucker on his shoulder.

"I think I've heard enough," she said. "I'm disappointed in you, Steek-55. I thought you were going to look after the minding module responsibly, not use it to make trouble for your fellow invaders."

"But, Miss Voob, it's true! Everyone knows Hex is bad luck! And now we know he's hiding something!"

"I said that's *enough*, Steek-55. Unless you want me to put you on gloop mixing duty. Now it's nearly break time. Everyone teleport down to the recreation zone before I lose my temper."

Hex found his way to the recreation zone in the end, although his tele-belt transported him to the relief zone, ingestion zone and the library before he finally managed to pick up the right signal. He spotted Opo and Dooper in a corner, and made his way over.

"Hex, you made it!" shouted Dooper. "Where have you been? Break's almost over!"

"Just a little tele-belt trouble . . . I've been all over the place. This thing does what it wants."

"Well, thanks for helping me out back there," said Dooper, and then turned an embarrassed shade of green. "Opo was just telling me what I did – in front of *everyone*. . ."

"Actually, you're a pretty good dancer!" joked Hex. "But . . . thanks for helping me, too – both of you. I really appreciate it."

"Believe me, it was my pleasure," said Opo, clenching her suckers.

"Well, it meant a lot," said Hex. "I know it doesn't do much for your popularity. I'm pretty much a joke around here, what with the Hex Effect and everything."

"Don't be silly, we *have* to stick together – we're the same," said Opo.

"We are?" said Hex.

"You bet!" bellowed Dooper. "Wait, how?"

"Look, I lost my mum in the invasion of the last Planet X," said Opo. "I know how hard it is. My brother's always been a pain in the nodes, but he had no right to make up stories about your dad. And it was especially horrid – even for him – to try and get your hopes up like that."

"Stink's a great big gwirm!" said Dooper. "I was a hatchling when I lost my mum and dad. I don't even remember them, but if someone said bad things about them – BOOM! They'd get a sucker sandwich right in the gills!"

Hex suddenly wondered if his friends might understand why he had to save his dad, even if it meant stopping the invasion of Earth.

Opo had already told Hex that she wasn't a fan of space invading, and they'd both lost so much because of it – much more than him. How much could they really like space invading, if it had cost them their parents?

"Hey, do you two want to come over to the orphanarium after school?" Dooper continued, "I've never had friends round before! We'll have the best time ever! We can play alien-in-the-middle and abduction and seek . . . and space invasers! Team Dooper, Hex and Opo, the best space invasers ever! BOOM!"

"BOOM!" shouted Opo with a giggle.

Hex's circulatory organ sank. In the end,

everything came back to space invading. Planetexians put space invading before *anything* – even families and friendship.

"Actually, um, I'm a bit busy tonight. Space invader stuff, you know how it is. Maybe another time," said Hex. He suddenly felt rather alone. At least his secret was safe, for now. But Hex knew it was only a matter of time before something else went horribly wrong.

Hex had to work out a plan of action, and there was only one planetexian who could help him now – his dad.

FOUND OUT

The rest of the morning passed without any other problems. Hex was so relieved that no one believed Steek that he didn't even mind a whole hour of abduction training. Even the Hex Effect seemed to be helping for a change – instead of teleporting him to the ingestion zone, he was transported to a quiet corridor – the perfect place to contact his dad in secret.

Hex checked no one was around and took his little robot out of his pocket.

"Keep watch for me, Glitch," he said, and Glitch rolled on to the floor with a "POP! POP!". Hex took a deep breath and turned on his P.A.D.

PING!

"Dad, are you there?"

There was a pause . . . then:

> HI, SON. HOW'S SCHOOL? TROUBLE-FREE, I HOPE?

"Not exactly – I just had my mind read by the meanest boy in the whole school! He knows you're alive!"

> MINDING MODULES, I'LL BET. I ALWAYS HATED THOSE THINGS. WHAT ELSE DID HE FIND OUT? DOES ANYONE ELSE SUSPECT ANYTHING?

"Well no, I don't think so. The minding module blew up before he could read any more of my thoughts, but—"

> SEE, I TOLD YOU THE HEX EFFECT WOULD COME IN HANDY. IT DOESN'T ALWAYS MESS THINGS UP. . .

"But it's only a matter of time! You're right, Dad – I can't stay here. I have to get off this stupid, invasion-obsessed planet before it's too late!"

YOU'RE MAKING A BRAVE CHOICE, SON, AND IN THE END, YOU'LL SEE THAT IT'S THE RIGHT ONE. EVERYTHING'S GOING TO BE FINE, MARK MY WORDS. WHEN YOU'RE SITTING HERE WITH LEMONADE AND CAKE, YOU'LL LOOK BACK AND REALIZE HOW LUCKY YOU ARE.

"I have no idea what you just said," said Hex. "What's lem and aiden-cake?"

UH, NEVER MIND, LET'S NOT GET OFF THE POINT. FIRST THINGS FIRST – YOU NEED A HYPERSAUCER.

"A *hypersaucer*? Where am I going to get one of those? They won't let us fly real hypersaucers! I mean, I know I *did* fly one, but that was all the Hex Effect's fault."

BELIEVE ME, HEX, AFTER TWENTY-TWO YEARS AT SPORG'S, I THOUGHT THE HEX EFFECT WAS TO BLAME TOO. BUT IN THE END, THAT'S WHAT BROUGHT ME TO EARTH, SAFE AND SOUND. NOW I HAVE A WHOLE NEW LIFE, FREE OF SPACE INVADING AND DISINTEGRATION.

"But I can't wait twenty-two years – I have to get out of here now!" said Hex.

YOUR MOTHER IS A HYPERSAUCER CAPTAIN, SHE MUST HAVE ACCESS TO THE HYPERSAUCER HANGARS. DO YOU THINK YOU COULD CONVINCE HER TO TAKE YOU ON A TOUR?

"Well . . . maybe, but what do I do when I get there? Mum's not going to just let me borrow a hypersaucer!" replied Hex.

YOU'RE PROBABLY RIGHT . . . I KNOW YOU'LL FIND A WAY – EVEN IF IT MEANS STEALING A HYPERSAUCER FROM THE EMPRESS HERSELF! I WISH I COULD HELP YOU MORE. TRUST IN THE HEX EFFECT, SON. I KNOW YOU DON'T BELIEVE IT NOW, BUT IT'S THE BEST CHANCE YOU HAVE.

"How can I trust it? It's been nothing but trouble ever since I started space invader school! I almost got disintegrated *again* today! Do you know how close Steek got to finding out what I did? I mean, I invaded the royal palace! I smashed up the empress's sentry-bots! I pretended to be an earthling! And then, to top it all off, I made the empress call off the invasion of Earth – while she was sitting on the toilet! What am I supposed to do if someone finds out?" cried Hex.

"Klik-kik-kik POP! POP! POP!" said Glitch, loudly. Hex turned slowly around to see him pointing to the right. There was Opo, standing in the corridor. She'd heard every word he'd said.

"Steek was right – he was right all along. . ." she said, quietly.

"Opo. . . I. . . I – " began Hex, but how could he possibly explain? Hex panicked, and did the first thing he could think of – he ran!

"Stop! Hex, stop!" cried Opo, chasing after Hex as he raced away. Hex ran as fast as his little green legs could carry him, down the corridor, then through a nearby portal into training zone 6. He looked around for another way out but there was nowhere to go, and he could already hear Opo's footsteps coming after him. He spotted a storage zone and raced inside to hide.

"Kik-POP?" said Glitch.

"Shhhh!" said Hex, covering Glitch's verbalizer with a sucker. He held his breath and waited, but after a minute or so, he began to wonder whether Opo had given up and gone straight to Headmaster Sporg.

He had to get out of there without anyone noticing him. He looked around for something, anything that he could use to disguise himself. There were dozens of shelves, each filled with hundreds of containers, all clearly marked: RAY-GUNS, PULSE-GRENADES,

DEFLECTION SHIELDS, MAGNA-BOOTS...
Everything a space invader in training could
need. Suddenly, something caught his eye.
A container marked HOLO-SUITS.

Hex shivered. He hadn't had much luck
with holo-suits. In fact, Hex's one and only
holo-suit experience had been probably
the craziest hour of his life. Then again, he
had ended up saving Earth from invasion.
He knew it was his only chance. He lifted
the crate down and took out a holo-suit. He
gulped down a deep breath and put it on.

"POP! Chik POP!" said Glitch, anxiously.

"I know, but what other choice do I have?"
replied Hex. He pulled the hood over his head
and tugged the zip all the way up. The holo-
suit flickered and Hex was transformed . . .
into a purple-skinned, ten-tentacled gwirm.

"POP! POP!" said Glitch in horror.

"Must have been left over from another
invasion. This is no good, I can't go walking

around as a gwirm, I'll be disintegrated on sight. If I could just recalibrate the imager somehow . . . where's the image modulizer?" said Hex. He reached under his armpits, then behind his knees, then on the soles of his feet. "Transponding nodules . . . phase array . . . diffusion circuits. . ." Finally, he inspected the tips of his suckers.

"There they are!" he cried. As Glitch looked on in disbelief, Hex clicked his suckers together, and the holo-suit image flickered and then changed! Within moments, Hex looked like a flat-tailed bundin.

"How do I look?" he said, looking down his long, scaly snout.

"Klik-ka-chik chik-ik!" said Glitch, shaking his head.

Hex clicked his suckers again, making him look like a many-headed mokkrul. Then again, disguising him as a blue-furred flox. Before long, the holo-suit had scrolled

through twenty disguises, from aliens of every size and shape to a planetexian police officer. Eventually he clicked his way to an assisto-bot disguise. Hex looked down at his thin, metal pincers.

"An assisto-bot will do nicely! They're all over the school – no one will look twice at me. Come on, Glitch."

Glitch rolled on to Hex's shoulder as Hex opened the storage zone door carefully and sneaked out. His disguise was perfect – he even whirred and clanked as he moved! Now all he had to do was to get out of the school and as far away as possible.

Hex walked down corridor after corridor, past training zone after training zone until he reached the ingestion zone. It was full of hungry children, all happily tucking into bowls of gloop. He spotted Dooper and Steek, but no Opo! Had she headed straight for Sporg's zone to tell him everything?

Hex fought every instinct to run, and slowly made his way through the ingestion zone. He was halfway to the door when Opo burst in behind him. She took one look at him and raced towards him! Hex was about to make a break for it, when she ran straight past.

"Dooper! Have you seen Hex?" she said, grabbing Dooper as he stuffed his feeding tube with gloop.

"Where's he gone now? I can't keep up with him!" laughed Dooper. "He's always teleporting off somewhere or other. Maybe he's squeezing in some extra space invaser training!"

Hex didn't wait for Opo to tell Dooper his terrible secret. He headed straight for the exit . . . but in his panic he failed to notice a glob of spilled gloop directly in his path.

SWlll-llP!

Hex's feet flew out from underneath him and he crashed to the floor! As he lay on the floor, dazed, Opo and Doopcr (and almost everyone else in the ingestion zone) turned to see what had happened. Hex scrambled to his feet and started running.

"Ka-chik chik POP POP?" asked a concerned Glitch.

"Shhh!" replied Hex. "Keep quiet, or we're as good as disintegrated!"

"Hex?" said Opo, recognizing Hex's voice. She spun around and along with everyone else, saw an assisto-bot dashing away. Everyone stared as it clambered over a table and out into the main hall.

Only one pupil looked down at the floor where the assisto-bot had slipped on gloop – *Steek*. He noticed something small and silver lying on the ground, and as he leaned down and picked it up, he realized that it was a P.A.D.

Steek turned it on and the P.A.D. pinged into life. He inspected it closely, wondering why an assisto-bot would have its own Personal Advice Device. Then, as he stared at the screen, Steek suddenly had his answer.

> HEX? ARE YOU THERE, SON? WHAT'S GOING ON?
> HAVE YOU BEEN FOUND OUT?

"Son?" said Steek. "I knew it . . . I knew it!"

HOW TO STEAL A HYPERSAUCER

Hex ran on to the huge landing platform outside the school, and then dashed to a nearby elevation tube and darted inside. He was immediately whisked up to a magna-bridge high above the school.

By now, Hex's mind was racing far faster than he was. Who had Opo told? Dooper? Headmaster Sporg? Maybe the police, or the empress herself? Whoever she'd told, Hex had run out of time – he had to get off Planet X, *today.*

"Klick-chik-ka-chik?" asked Glitch.

"I don't know!" replied Hex, staring out of the window. "I don't know where I'm going. . ."

Hex raced across the bridge and hopped on to a fast moving conveyor belt. He shuffled between the crowds of planetexians going about their business, until he was dwarfed on either side by the vast, gleaming towers of New X City.

Finally, exhausted, he spotted a magna-tram pulling into a nearby waiting platform. He jumped off the conveyor belt and hurried on to the tram just as the doors closed. He stared at the vid-screen above his seat, trying to look like any normal assisto-bot riding a magna-tram would. Advert after advert flashed up in front of his face.

As the magna-tram sped through New X City, Hex realized he no longer had any idea where he was. He had travelled further than he had ever been . . . but he was no closer to having an escape plan. Then, as if on cue, an advert flashed up on the vid-screen in front of him.

This was the answer! Hex didn't need to steal a hypersaucer – he could buy one! All he needed was 9,999,999 quix! Hex reached into his pocket and searched around for his pocket money. He had never been very good at saving. He tended to spend everything he had on spare parts for his robot creations.

"Two quix and twenty-four voots," he said, staring at the six tiny coins in his sucker. Hex sighed and looked at Glitch. "Only nine million, nine-hundred and ninety-nine thousand, nine-hundred and ninety-seven quix and seventy-six voots to go."

"POP-chik-ik?" asked Glitch, hopefully.

"Not even if I save up for a thousand years," replied Hex with a sigh. "There's no way I'm going to get a hypersaucer, unless. . ." Hex remembered what his dad had told him, about stealing a hypersaucer. It seemed impossible, and more than a little wrong, but then he *did* have his dad's permission . . . and it was better than being disintegrated. He had no choice – he was going to have to borrow one of Honest Zeeb's hypersaucers to get to Earth.

Hex waited for stop 2395 and hopped

off the magna-tram. He followed the signs for the emporium until he caught sight of a large, dome-like building, surrounded by a vast, open forecourt. It was filled with hypersaucer after hypersaucer, thirty or more – all gleaming silver and polished so hard that Hex could see his reflection in the surface. The only problem was, no one was going to let a boy (or even a boy disguised as an assisto-bot) get close enough to a hypersaucer to fly it away. He ducked behind a hypersaucer and started clicking his suckers! In an instant, the holo-suit began shifting image again.

"Glitch, tell me when I get to something I can use," mumbled Hex as he clicked through alien after alien and robot after robot. Glitch inspected each camouflage, one after the other, and kept shaking his head. Finally, Glitch popped and nodded in excitement.

"This one? What is it? What do I look like?" asked Hex, and then caught his reflection in the hypersaucer's hull. He almost jumped out of his holo-suit. . .

He looked like Empress Valoona.

HONEST ZEEB'S
HYPERSAUCER EMPORIUM

"No way! I am not pretending to be the empress! I'm in enough trouble as it is!" protested Hex, staring at his reflection. He looked exactly like Empress Valoona, complete with short, fat body, bulbous head and squeezed-on crown. Hex tried to get the image to change, but no matter how many times he clicked his suckers, he remained stuck as the empress.

"POP! Klik-ka-chik-POP!" said Glitch, approvingly.

"But I could get disintegrated!" began Hex. Glitch just stared at him. "Yeah, you're right . . . what's new?" Hex added. He sidled out from behind the hypersaucer and made his way towards the emporium entrance.

"OK, act natural," Hex whispered to himself, sneaking inside. "And . . . empress-like."

Hex crept into the emporium, trying not to be noticed by any of the other planetexians milling around. Hex spotted a short, fat planetexian behind a counter. He had a surprisingly small brain-sack and was talking into a hear lobe-mounted communicator, so loudly that he could almost have been heard from outer space.

"Nah, listen mate – I ain't talking about your run of the mill X7 or X8 model – no, no, no. I'm talking top of the range – the sort of saucer that turns heads and makes brain-sacks throb with jealousy. Your neighbours will turn red with envy when they see you pulling up in the X9! You want to know the long, short and green of it? You can't afford *not* to buy this hypersaucer! As true as the sky is pink – you need this hypersaucer in your life, or my name's not Honest Zeeb!"

"Uh, excuse me," said Hex, sheepishly, in his very best empress voice. Zeeb didn't even turn around – he just raised his sucker in the air and carried on talking into his communicator.

"Now listen, I've got an X9 in the lot right now – one careless owner, 456,000,000 light years on the clock, all the trimmings. . . Why don't you pop by today, give it a test-fly?"

"Um . . . I'd like to buy a hypersaucer, please," whispered Hex, even more timidly.

"I *said*, keep your antenna on – I ain't an eight-armed octolillo, I've only got the one set of suckers," said Zeeb, abruptly, still not bothering to look up.

Glitch shook his head and reached out a pincer, pinching the salesman hard on the hear lobe.

"YOW!" squealed Zeeb, spinning around.

"Here, what on Planet X do you think you're—"

He froze.

"You're – you're – Your Majesty!" Zeeb squealed and immediately dropped to his knees. "Forgive me, Your Majestic Greenness, I didn't see you there! A thousand million billion apologies!"

"Uh, not to worry ... no need to make a fuss," replied Hex as everyone in the emporium turned to see what all the commotion was about. The second they laid eyes on the empress, they too, fell to their knees! Hex tried not to smile. This might be easier than he'd thought. . .

"How can I be of service, Your Marvellous Majesticness? Would you like an emporium tourium? I mean, a pour of the emtorium? I mean, a *tour of the emporium*?" stumbled Zeeb. "Everything's above-board and green, of course! This is just a hobby really –

something to do between space invasions! You know what it's like – got to make a living, got to feed the hatchlings. . ."

"Uh, I'd like – I mean, your empress would like a hypersaucer," said Hex, trying to sound empress-like. "The best one you've got."

"Of course! Take whichever one you want! Free of charge, of course! Everything you see belongs to you anyway, Your Empressness!" said Zeeb, guiding Hex outside to the hypersaucer lot. "How about this X-8500 – it's been through two invasions and flies like a dream! But what am I thinking? You want the best of the best!"

"Uh, yes, the best of the best would be . . . best," said Hex, noticing a small crowd of onlookers and floating vid-bots starting to gather outside the emporium. The last thing he wanted was to appear on a news-vid!

"Nothing else would do for Her Megajestic Empress!" said Zeeb, continuing to bow as he directed Hex to the largest, most impressive looking hypersaucer in the lot. "The X10 – fresh from the invasion of this Planet X! Now I only have two of these, but you're welcome to them both!"

"This looks perfect!" said Hex, excitedly. "But can I just check . . . would this hypersaucer get me, or someone else, all the way to – oh, I don't know – Earth?"

"*Earth*, Your Majesty?" said Zeeb, suspiciously. "As in, *Planet* Earth?"

"Yes, yes, Planet Earth – the uh, the stinking mudball that I was going to invade but then didn't – that one," said a nervous Hex, as the crowds outside grew larger. "I was just curious, you know, in case I fancied a holiday, or . . . a day trip, or something. . ."

"Well, no, of course not, Your Most Masterful Empressness," said Zeeb, as though he was being tested. "None of these hypersaucers can get off the planet – by your own royal command."

"Wh-what? What do mean, *none* of them?" asked Hex.

"Well, no. Every second-hand hypersaucer

has its hyperdriver removed – just like you ordered, so it can't . . . I mean, so no one can. . ." began Zeeb, awkwardly.

". . .*escape*," finished Hex, suddenly realizing what Zeeb meant. He looked around at the sea of hypersaucers. They were useless to him. They couldn't even get him into space, never mind all the way to Earth!

"Not that anyone would want to escape!" said Zeeb quickly. "Not when life as a planetexian is so glorious! All hail Your Majesty! All hail space invasion! If in doubt, disintegrate!"

"No, no, no. . ." said Hex, despairing. "You mean, you don't have *any* hypersaucers that can get me to Earth?"

"No offence, Your Most Majestic Empress, but don't you have a whole *fleet* of invasion-ready hypersaucers at your disposal – I mean, brand new ones, with hyperdrivers and everything?" said Zeeb, daring to inspect

Hex a little more closely.

"What? Uh, yes, of course I do!" said Hex, panicking about blowing his cover. "Don't question the empress! Do you want to be disintegrated?"

"N-no, Your Majesty! No, I didn't mean anything! Forgive me, Your Majesty!" screamed Zeeb, throwing himself at Hex's feet, again.

"Yeah, well, OK then – just don't do it again," said Hex. "Now, can you get a hypersaucer with a working hyperdriver or not?"

"Well, I might have the odd one. . ." said Zeeb, uneasily. "Not that I sell them you understand! I just . . . haven't got round to altering them. I mean, who'd want a hypersaucer that could go into space? Who'd want to leave Planet X? No one, that's who! Everyone loves it here!"

"But if I wanted to leave. . ." began Hex, cautiously.

"These babies would take you anywhere you wanted to go! Perfect for, uh, day trips," said Zeeb, looking a little suspicious. Hex straightened his holo-crown and tried to look regal.

"I'll take one," he said.

ESCAPE FROM PLANET X (1ST ATTEMPT)

Zeeb led the disguised Hex through the emporium and into his office. He reached up to a picture of two plump planetexian children mounted on the wall, and slid it aside. Behind it was a large, green button. Zeeb pressed it and the wall split apart to reveal a secret elevation tube!

"This way, Your Most Wondrous Majesticness," said Zeeb, guiding Hex into the tube. Hex stepped nervously into the beam of anti-gravity, and slowly began to descend. Before long, the elevation tube deposited Hex and Zeeb in a huge, underground hangar. Hex took a sharp breath into his gills – it was full of hypersaucers, perhaps fifteen of them. They weren't polished or pretty, and many had blast marks and damage from previous invasions.

"Amazing. . ." said Hex, as he wandered into the hangar. "And they all have hyperdrivers? What are they used for?"

"Uh, well, the thing is. . ." Zeeb began awkwardly, his brain-sack dripping with nervous sweat. Hex remembered what Opo had told him, about there being *loads* of planetexians who didn't want to be space invaders. Suddenly, everything started to make a strange sort of sense.

"Do you sell these? Do other planetexians use them to escape?" continued Hex, sternly. "Your empress wants to know! I command you tell me! Has anyone ever escaped from Planet X?"

"They . . . they have tried. They come to me, wanting to buy space-worthy hypersaucers. . ." confessed Zeeb, hoping he wasn't sentencing himself to disintegration for selling illegal hypersaucers. "But no one's actually managed to escape, of course. Your hypersaucer fleet makes sure of that – they shoot down anything that tries!"

"Wait, so no one's escaped? No one *at all*?" asked Hex in horror.

"Of course not! Everyone knows you can't escape from Planet X! But people just keep trying – I suppose I'm selling a dream," replied Zeeb with a nervous laugh.

Hex felt rather strange. All this time he had thought he was the only creature on Planet X who didn't want to be a space invader . . . but Opo had been right all along – there were more. Hex wondered how many had tried and failed. Could his father really be the only planetexian who had ever managed to escape? Had it been the Hex Effect that had carried him through the black hole to safety? Might the same be true for Hex? After a moment, he took a deep breath and made up his mind.

"I'll take that one," he said, finally. "Don't bother wrapping it, I'll fly it out of here."

"Very good, Your Majesticness!" said Zeeb, delighted that he hadn't been sentenced to disintegration. He grabbed a set of keys from a hook on the wall and then waved them at the hypersaucer. With a **bip-bip!** the hypersaucer door opened and a ramp descended to the floor.

"Would you like to look around first? I could throw in some extras – no charge of course! Air conditioning, suckers-free P.A.D. lock, fluffy dice. . ."

"No thanks, I'm in a bit of a rush, actually. Lots of empress stuff to do," said Hex. He was so close to escaping, he could almost smell the far reaches of orbit. He reached out for the key, but just as he was about to grab it, the image of the empress's fat sucker *flickered*. Hex quickly hid his sucker behind his back and looked up at a blinking Zeeb.

"You – yuh – wuh – " blurted Zeeb, staring at Hex, his mouth wide open and a disturbing look of surprise on his face.

"I'd, uh, I'd better be off then," said Hex, waving his sucker. "The work of a busy empress is never done . . . and that's me, the empress!"

It was then he spotted his sucker didn't look like a sucker at all – not even a fat, empress's sucker – it looked like a tentacle! No, a scaly claw! No, a feathery wing! The holo-suit was going haywire!

"What . . . what on Planet X *are* you?" cried Zeeb.

"Well, goodbye then!" cried Hex, urgently! He tried to grab the key, but Zeeb held it above his head.

"You're not the empress!" he shouted, and grabbed Hex by the neck! There was a crunching sound as the holo-suit's image stabilizer fizzled and hissed, and a split-second later Hex looked like Hex again.

"You crafty nudlork, it's a holo-suit! You're just a little runt!" growled Zeeb, drawing a ray-gun from his tele-belt and pointing it in Hex's face.

"AAH! Wait! Please! It's . . . it's not what it looks like!" gasped Hex, as Zeeb tightened his sucker-grip.

"Chik-POP!" pleaded Glitch.

"I almost gave you my best hypersaucer! I . . . I kissed your feet! You filthy slipe! Don't you know it's a disintegrate-able offence to disguise yourself as the empress?" said Zeeb, pressing his ray-gun into Hex's face.

"Please . . . just . . . need . . . hypersaucer. . .!" gasped Hex, desperately.

"It's too late for that, you little skutchweed,"

snarled Zeeb. "Now you'd better be green with me: does anyone else know you're here?"

"No . . . no one at all . . . I promise!" cried Hex.

"Good, that'll make disintegrating you a whole lot easier. . ." Zeeb said, but as he was about to pull the ray-gun trigger, Glitch jumped off Hex's shoulder and on to Zeeb's brain-sack! He started rolling around his head, grabbing hold of whatever he could – antenna, hear lobes, even gills!

"Get off me!" shouted Zeeb, plucking Glitch off and throwing him across the hangar. Glitch bounced off a hypersaucer and fell motionless to the ground.

"Glitch!" cried Hex.

"Right, no more messing around!" boomed Zeeb. "Give my regards to the Little Green Man in the Sky. . ."

"Hey!" came a cry from behind Zeeb. Hex turned to see two figures rushing out of the bottom of the elevation tube. It was Opo and Dooper!

"Who on Planet X. . .? What is this, a school trip?" said Zeeb. He pointed his ray-gun straight at them . . . but Dooper had Hex's ray-gun. As Hex screamed "Get out of here! Run!", Zeeb and Dooper both fired.

ZWAAARK! ZWAAARK!

RAY-GUNS AND REVELATIONS

The beam from Zeeb's ray-gun streaked across the hangar, singeing Dooper's antenna, but Dooper's own shot hit Zeeb squarely in the chest! He staggered backwards, his head spinning, and then slumped to the floor and immediately started snoring.

"Good shot, Dooper!" said Opo. "Still, he's only stunned – let's not hang around too long."

"What are you doing here?" asked Hex, panicking. "How did you find me?"

"Well, I thought I heard your voice back in the ingestion zone but I couldn't see you . . . then when I saw an assisto-bot I knew something wasn't right – Miss Voob told us they were all working on the empress's super sentry-bot. I realized you'd probably done something crazy . . . like disguised yourself with a holo-suit," replied Opo.

"It seemed like a good idea at the time," said Hex, looking down at the wrecked holo-suit.

"Well I decided to go after you, and Dooper agreed to help," said Opo.

"Well we *are* Team Dooper, Hex and Opo – BOOM!" bellowed Dooper.

"The hardest part was following you all the way here – we nearly lost you after you got off the magna-tram. But then I saw a news-vid of Empress Valoona trying to buy a hypersaucer from Honest Zeeb's Hypersaucer Emporium and sort of guessed it might be you – especially as the empress never leaves her palace," Opo said. "Then when we sneaked in and found the elevation tube, it all made sense."

"Team Dooper and Opo to the rescue!" said Dooper.

"Are you going to tell everyone about me?" asked Hex, panicking. "Please, don't! I don't want to be disintegrated!"

"No! No, of course not! Why would we want to see you disintegrated?" replied Opo. "I told you, we're your *friends*. I mean, we *did* just save your life, you know. . ."

"Sorry, it's just . . . well, I thought if you knew what I'd done. . ." began Hex, picking up a dazed, slightly dented Glitch.

"Hex, I keep telling you – you're not the only planetexian who doesn't want to be a space invader. I hate it more than anything! But nobody talks about the downside, do they? Nobody talks about losing your family or moving around all the time or never being able to do anything that's not about blowing stuff up! Nobody talks about anything except how great space invading is," said Opo.

"Well, I think it's amazing what you did – if I had the chance to save my mum like you saved your dad, I'd have done exactly the same thing."

"Wait a minute, *neither* of you want to be space invasers? Really? Honestly at all? Not even a teeny little bit of a bit?" asked Dooper, a look of horror on his face.

"Sorry, Dooper. I didn't know how to tell you," said Hex. "I know how much space invading means to you – I mean, it's all you ever talk about. . ."

"But – but – but –" began Dooper. "But this is great! I thought I was the only one!"

"The only one. . . What?" asked Hex.

"The only planetexian who hated space invasing! I thought there was something wrong with me! Space invasing, space invasing, all the time! Why do you think I always shout about space invasing so much?"

"You don't want to be a space invader? Really?" said Hex, not quite believing what he was hearing.

"I hate it! I just *really* wanted to fit in. . ." replied Dooper. "Hey, we could form a new team! Team Dooper, Hex and Opo, the secretly-don't-want-to-be-space-invasers!"

Hex felt as though a weight was being lifted off his brain-sack . . . and thoroughly guilty for not trusting his friends in the first place.

"I'm sorry I ran off like that," said Hex. "I thought if I could steal a hypersaucer I could get away before everyone found out what I'd done."

"Well, then, it looks like we found you just in time," said Opo. "Don't you know what happens to planetexians who try and escape?"

"Yeah, Honest Zeeb let me in on the secret," said Hex.

"Hex, the only way you're going to get disintegrated is if you get on that hypersaucer. Your secret is safe with us, right Dooper?

"Right! We're Team Dooper, Hex and Opo!" hollered Dooper.

"Thanks. I appreciate it, I really do," said Hex, slipping the dazed Glitch into his pocket. "Now let's get out of here before Zeeb wakes up."

Hex ushered Opo and Dooper into the elevation tube and then hurried out of the emporium. By now, there were planetexians swarming all over the place, eager for a glimpse of their empress. Hex, Dooper and Opo slipped into the crowds and were soon on a magna-tram heading across New X City.

P.A.D. LUCK

As the magna-tram made its way through the city, the vid-screens were full of stories of the empress making her first ever appearance outside her emerald palace.

> **EMPRESS LEAVES PALACE FOR THE FIRST TIME!**

> **EMPRESS SEEN BUYING SECOND-HAND HYPERSAUCER!**

> **EMPRESS SAYS, "IT WASN'T ME! I'D NEVER MINGLE WITH COMMON FOLK!"**

Opo giggled and prodded Hex in the ribs. Hex managed a smile, and had to admit that he felt better than he had even before starting space invader school. He may not have escaped from Planet X, but now he wasn't even sure that he wanted to leave. Finally, he knew there really were planetexians like him. He knew he wasn't alone.

Three conveyor belts and a skybus trip later, Hex was home. He waved to his friends as he hopped off the skybus, and they gave him the suckers-up. Hex walked through the portal with a broad grin on his face.

"Well, someone's had a good day! And you know what they say – a happy invader is a better invader," said his mother as Hex wandered cheerfully into the ingestion zone. "So, how was school?"

"Oh, you know Mum, same old, same old," said Hex.

"Well, did you hear about the empress? She was seen at a hypersaucer emporium, in the middle of New X City! Can you imagine?"

"No, I hadn't heard – too busy training, I suppose," smirked Hex. He gulped down a bowl of gloop and made his way to his zone. He took Glitch out of his pocket and made sure his robot didn't have any permanent damage.

"How are you feeling?" he said as he popped out a dent that was squashing Glitch's gyros.

"Klik-ka-chik POP!" said Glitch, with relief. He looked around and added, "Chik-kik-ka-chik-ik?"

"No, we're not in Zeep's hypersaucer emporium, or in outer space for that matter. I decided we might stay here for a while."

"Chik-POP! Clik-POP!"

"No, I just feel like maybe . . . maybe I have a reason to stay," Hex replied, staring out of his window at the three planetexian moons. "Speaking of which, I should probably break the news to Dad. . ."

Hex reached down to his tele-belt for his P.A.D. but it wasn't there. He checked all round his tele-belt, then the floor, then every container, drawer, nook and cranny in his zone.

"Where is it? WHERE IS IT?" he shrieked in panic. "WHERE IS MY P.A.D.?!"

"Ka-chik POP! POP! POP!" said Glitch.

"How can I be calm? My dad is on that P.A.D.! What if I never find it? I'll never be able to speak to him again! Or worse, what if someone else finds it? I didn't delete Dad's messages! Everything he's ever sent me is still on there!" he cried, hysterically. "When did I last have it? I remember speaking to Dad in the corridor at school . . . but I've been all over the city since then! It could be *anywhere!*"

"POP! Chik! POP!" Glitch said, sternly.

"You're right. You're right, deep gill-breaths . . . I need to calm down," said Hex, pacing back and forth. "I mean, it's got to be *somewhere*, right? And why would anyone care about a lost P.A.D.? They probably wouldn't look at it twice. I have to retrace my steps. I have to find it, now!"

"Have to find what?" said his mother. She was standing in the doorway, her suckers on her hips.

"Mum! Hi! H-how long have you been listening? I mean, standing there?" asked Hex.

"Long enough," she said, sternly. "Now, you have 3.2 seconds to tell me *exactly* what's going on."

"I – I don't – uh . . . nothing," said Hex, but he knew it was too late. His mother had heard everything. She knew about his dad. His secret was well and truly out.

"Don't lie to me, Hex-37 – I heard what you were saying," she said. "You've lost your P.A.D., haven't you?"

"What? I mean, yeah, I did. . ." said Hex, quickly.

"Oh, Hex, what have I told you about looking after your things?" said his mother. "How can you expect to be a space invader if you can't take responsibility for your Personal Advice Device?"

She hadn't heard him talking about his dad! Hex grinned involuntarily.

"And you can wipe that smirk off your face," continued his mother. "It may not seem like a big deal to you, but P.A.D.s don't grow on trees you know. That little machine is one of a kind!"

"You can say that again," murmured Hex.

"Well, it's much too late to go looking for it now, and it's bound to be at school somewhere. It's not like you've been wandering around New X City, now is it?" she said.

"No, Mum!" said Hex, crossing his suckers.

STEEK'S REVENGE

Despite managing to keep the truth about his misadventures from his mum, Hex didn't sleep a wink – he was too busy worrying about his lost P.A.D. He stared out of the window and thought about his dad, hundreds of light years away and no doubt worried sick. Before long, Hex had worried through the entire night and it was time for school. He dragged himself out of his slumber pod before T.K. had a chance to whisk him out with a pincer, and stared at his bowl of gloop until the skybus arrived. As he hopped on, he could already hear Dooper shouting his name.

"Hex! I saved you a seat! Team Dooper, Hex and Opo, reporting for duty!" bellowed Dooper from the back of the bus. Hex shuffled down and squeezed in next to his friend.

"Another great day of space invaser training! I can't wait to disintegrate stuff! BOOM!" said Dooper, and then gave him a wink and a nudge. "Yep! Space invasing! That's what I love! BOOM!"

"How are you doing, Hex?" asked Opo from the seat behind him.

"Terrible . . . I've lost my P.A.D.!" whispered Hex.

"Your P.A.D.?" said Dooper and Opo together. "But where did – how did – when did –"

"I forgot to delete my messages! If anyone finds my P.A.D., they'll discover everything!"

"What are you three whispering about?"

said Steek, leaning over the chair in front of Hex with a grin on his face.

"Wh-what? Nothing!" said Hex, quickly.

"Mind your own business, Steek! Can't you just keep your antenna out of other people's conversations for once?" said Opo.

"Yeah, get lost, Stink," said Dooper.

"POP! POP!" said Glitch, joining in from Hex's pocket.

"I'm so sorry to interrupt – my mistake, do carry on," said Steek, politely, and sat back in his chair.

"What's he being so nice for?" whispered Hex. "Did he have a brain-sack transplant or something?"

"No idea. . ." said Opo, suspiciously.

Before long, the skybus landed outside the school and the pupils clambered eagerly off. For once, Hex pushed to the front of the queue, desperate to look for his P.A.D. before school started.

"OK, we'll split up," said Hex, as the children gathered in the main hall. "Opo, you search training zone 6 and the storage zone. Dooper, you look in the ingestion zone, and I'll search the corridors. If we don't find it before the first lesson, we'll start again at break. . ."

"I wouldn't bother, if I were you, said Steek, whispering into Hex's hear lobe. "You'll never find it."

Hex froze. "Never find what?" he asked, nervously.

"Why, your P.A.D., of course," said Steek, as the doors of the main hall slid shut. "Oh, I'm sorry, was I listening in again?"

"My – my P.A.D.?" whimpered Hex, turning around to face Steek. "Why, have . . . have you seen it?"

"Did I forget to mention? I found it in the ingestion zone, in a puddle of gloop."

"You found it?" squealed Hex.

"And then I happened to look at all the messages in your inbox. And guess what? I was right all along. Daddy's *alive*. And that's not all I found out. You've been a busy boy, Hex. . ."

Hex took a sharp breath. Steek knew. He knew *everything*.

"Where . . . where is my P.A.D.?" he asked in a small, desperate voice, hoping he wasn't going to get the answer he was expecting.

"Oh, I'm afraid I've already given it to Headmaster Sporg," said Steek, with a grin.

Hex suddenly felt dizzy, and his brain-sack started to ache. He remembered the sensation immediately. His mind was being probed!

"HEX-37!" came the cry, so loudly that it almost shook the walls. The crowd of gathered children immediately parted. It was just like Hex's dream. Hex peered to the far end of the hall, to see Headmaster Sporg on his floating podium. He was wearing a minding module on his head.

"I didn't believe it at first," said Headmaster Sporg, holding up a small, silver object. "But when Steek came to me with your P.A.D., I had to find out for myself. Because you see, the mind never lies . . . and I've just read yours!"

"Please, I—" began Hex, his whole world crashing around him like a malfunctioning hypersaucer.

"SILENCE! Never has one planetexian committed so many disintegrate-able crimes! Communication with other planets! Stealing a hypersaucer! Attacking the city! Teleporting into the empress's palace! And, worst of all, blackmailing the empress into calling off the invasion of Earth!"

The schoolchildren gasped in unison, hardly able to believe their hear lobes.

"Well, Hex-37?" continued Headmaster

Sporg. "What do you have to say for yourself?"

"I just wanted to help my dad. . ." whimpered a defeated Hex.

"SILENCE! I have no interest in hearing what you have to say for yourself! I have just given the signal to alert the empress. I suspect she will want to disintegrate you personally!"

"Ha!" guffawed Steek, unable to contain his joy.

"Steek, you slimy, scum-gilled little gwirm!" growled Opo. "How *could* you?"

"SILENCE! You will be taken to the empress's palace – under the watchful eye of the authorities," Headmaster Sporg said, as the hall was bathed in the familiar blue light of a teleporter. The air shimmered around Hex and a second later, four planetexian police officers had teleported into the hall! The officers surrounded him, their ray-guns drawn.

"Hex-37, you're under arrest!" shouted the police captain.

"Please! Wait! I can explain. . ." began Hex, cowering in fear.

"SILENCE!" yelled Headmaster Sporg. "Oh, except you, officers! You carry on!"

"Hex-37, you are to be delivered to the palace of Her Majestic Green, the Empress Valoona XIII, for immediate disintegration!" said the police captain.

"I told you you'd end up getting disintegrated!" laughed Steek. Opo turned around and swung her sucker into his face.

BLAM!

"Oh, shut up, Steek!" she said, as he fell to the floor, clutching his jaw.

As the police officers guided Hex towards the exit, Dooper stepped forward and unclipped his ray-gun from his belt.

"Nobody move, or you're all going BOOM!"

"No, Dooper, don't!" yelled Hex, as Dooper

strode towards the officers. They immediately started laughing.

"Pointing a ray-gun at a planetexian police officer is a disintegrate-able offence, tubby," laughed the captain. "Do you want to join your friend as a pile of dust?"

The officers aimed their ray-guns at Dooper, but he didn't stop. He just kept walking straight towards them, his ray-gun pointed at them.

"Drop the gun, fatso! I mean it, that's an order!" shouted the captain, now a little nervous.

"Dooper, please, do as he says!" cried Opo.

"Last chance, kid – you can't take us all on. There are four of us, and only one of you," said the captain, sternly.

"I disintegrated fifty-eight target-bots in thirty-nine seconds, and they were all firing back," said Dooper, proudly.

"Fifty-eight? Really? I've only ever managed fourteen – and that took a whole hour," mumbled the captain, his antenna glowing blue with terror. "Shoot him, men! Shoot him now!"

"Really, Captain? He's just some fat kid," said one of the officers.

"How many times – I have overactive elbow glands!" cried Dooper, and fired.

ZWAARK! ZWAARK! ZWAAARK! ZWAAAAAAARK!

"Huh ... target-bots move *much* faster than people – that was easy!" said Dooper as all four officers fell to the floor, stunned!

"OK, now we're *really* in trouble," whispered Hex to Opo.

"Enough! I have never seen such un-invader-like behaviour in all my life!" screamed Headmaster Sporg, zooming towards Hex on his podium. "I'll deliver you to the empress myself – who knows, maybe she'll promote me to *super* headmaster, if there is such a job."

"Hey Sporg!" came a cry. Headmaster Sporg and Hex turned around to see Dooper, pointing his ray-gun.

"Don't you dare point that thing at me! It's one thing to shoot an officer of planetexian law, but I am a *teacher*!" shouted Headmaster Sporg. "Now, put down the ray-gun, this instant, or else I'll—"

"Boom," whispered Dooper, a wide grin spreading across his face.

ZWAAAAAARK!

THE SUPER SENTRY-BOT

With a single stun-beam from Dooper's ray-gun, Headmaster Sporg fell to the floor, well and truly stunned. Dooper twirled the ray-gun around his sucker.

"I could get used to this . . . maybe there are some parts of space invasing I *do* like," he said under his breath.

"Thanks Dooper!" said Hex. "I'll take that!" he added, prising his P.A.D. from Headmaster Sporg's sucker.

HEX? HEX, ARE YOU THERE? WHAT'S GOING ON? I HAVEN'T
BEEN ABLE TO REACH YOU FOR AGES –
DID YOUR P.A.D. MALFUNCTION OR SOMETHING?

"Yeah, *or something*," said Hex. "Don't worry, I'll tell you later – on Earth, hopefully! I'm on my way, Dad!"

Hex and Dooper dashed down the hall and were quickly joined by Opo as they raced on to the landing platform outside.

"FREEZE!"

Hex looked up. A police skycar hovered in the air above them!

"ATTENTION, HEX-37. THIS IS THE PLANET X POLICE! YOU ARE UNDER ARREST! SURRENDER IMMEDIATELY SO THAT WE CAN TAKE YOU TO THE EMPRESS FOR DISINTEGRATION ... OR BE DISINTEGRATED! YOU HAVE FIVE ... NO, THREE SECONDS TO COMPLY!"

"We surrender! Please, don't shoot!" cried Hex, waving his suckers.

"Hey, Sergeant, does that look like an 'I surrender!' wave or a 'get lost!' wave to you?" said the police skycar pilot.

"Hard to tell . . . he does have a 'please don't shoot' look on his face," said the sergeant, peering through his viewscreen. "Then again, he could be bluffing. You'd better double-check. . ."

"ATTENTION, HEX-37!" said the pilot through the loudspeaker. "ARE YOU DOING THE 'I SURRENDER' WAVE OR THE 'GET STUFFED' WAVE? WE'RE TRYING TO WORK OUT WHETHER TO DISINTEGRATE YOU OR NOT."

"What? No! I mean, yes! I mean, the first one!" screamed Hex.

"Not exactly a definitive response," said the sergeant. "Tell you what, let's disintegrate him just a bit. An arm or a leg or something. . ."

"Yes, sir!" said the pilot. He reached out a sucker for the DISINTEGRATE button, when a blue glow of teleportation energy appeared behind the police skycar. Something was teleporting in!

A moment later, a huge shape appeared on the landing platform – and Hex saw immediately that it was much worse than the police. It was a robot – and it was *huge*. Hex recognized it from the news-vids.

The super sentry-bot!

"STOP! THE TRAITOR IS MINE!" boomed the super sentry-bot, swatting the police skycar out of the way with a massive pincer and sending it crashing to the ground!

"I think it's talking about you," whispered Dooper.

Hex stared up at the gargantuan robot hovered in the air above them. For a moment, Hex was lost in terrified admiration . . . until he noticed a panel on the robot's chest slide open to reveal a huge holo-screen. It began to flicker and a second later an image of Empress Valoona appeared.

"Uh-oh," said Hex.

"Well, well . . . Hex-37 – at last we meet!" squealed the empress, excitedly. "Although, we've met before, haven't we? When you invaded my emerald palace, disguised as an earthling!"

"Please . . . Your Majesty, I mean, Your Empressness, I mean . . . I didn't mean to . . . it was the—" began Hex.

"So, what do think of my *super* sentry-bot? Pretty nifty, isn't he? Especially the in-built voice control and holo-screen – I can command my unstoppable robot guardian, from the comfort of my emerald living zone! I get to enjoy all the disintegration without ever even leaving the palace!" said the empress, proudly.

"That's great," said Hex, trying to be as polite as possible.

"I *know* it's great, and it was completed just in time to disintegrate you! Well, the instructions did say to charge its anti-matter battery overnight, but how much power is it going to need to get rid of one little boy?" cackled the empress. "Let's find out, shall we? Super sentry-bot, destroy him!"

"RUN! Find cover! It's me she's after!" shouted Hex as the super sentry-bot silently obeyed its controller, swinging a massive pincer! It smashed through the wall of the school, sending up screams of terror from the children inside. Opo and Dooper dashed across the landing platform and headed for the crashed skycar. They ducked behind it just as the two police officers scrambled out and ran for their lives.

"Uh, do you think this is a good place to – wait, where's Hex?" asked Dooper, peering over the skycar. "He didn't follow us! That boom-bot is right on top of him! We have to help him!"

"I know, I know! I'm thinking!" replied

Opo, banging the skycar with her clenched suckers. It was then she peered inside, and noticed the keys were still in the activation slot. . .

By running in another direction, Hex was now well and truly cornered by the super sentry-bot. He stared up in horror as the super sentry-bot loomed over him.

"There's nowhere to hide, traitor!" cried the empress. "I'm going to disintegrate you, piece by piece! No one makes a fool of Empress Valoona! No one!"

"Klik-POP?" said Glitch, poking his head out of Hex's pocket. He pointed at Hex's tele-belt, which had started to rumble and spark.

"Not again! What's *wrong* with this thing? I didn't set it to receive! It's not even – uh oh," replied Hex, as he stared down the barrel of a death ray-cannon.

"Let this be a lesson to all those who would betray me!" screamed the empress.

ZWAAAAAARK!

"Missed! Where'd he go?" screeched the empress, as Hex de-materialized in a flash of blue light! He had teleported! A second later, the empress saw Hex re-materialize a few metres away. "Aha! There you are!"

ZWAAARK!

Another death ray shot out of the super sentry-bot's cannons, but Hex teleported again, re-materializing nearby.

"Stop doing that! I can't disintegrate you if you don't hold still!" hissed the empress.

"I'm not doing anything!" cried Hex. "It's this tele-belt! I—"

ZWARK! ZWAARK! ZWAAAARK!

Hex teleported again and again, avoiding death ray after death ray!

"HOLD STILL TRAITOR!! YOUR EMPRESS COMMANDS YOU TO HOLD STILL!"

screamed the empress!

"It's the Hex Effect . . . I think it's trying to save me!" said Hex, re-materializing elsewhere on the landing platform. Then, just as he was beginning to think his dad might be right about trusting the Hex Effect, he teleported and re-materialized . . . in mid-air, hundreds of metres above the ground!

"Or maybe not," he muttered as he started to fall!

"Ha HA!" cried the empress as she watched Hex plummet! "Goodbye, traitor! You've sealed your own fate!"

"YAAAAAAAAAH!" screamed Hex – and "POP! Chik! POP!" screamed Glitch – as they saw the ground coming towards them at high speed. Hex's short, eventful life flashed before his eyes, especially the really terrible bits, after he had started space invader school.

As he was about to hit the ground, he

remembered thinking his dad must have been wrong after all about the Hex Effect, and wished more than ever that he'd had a chance to see him again.

KRUMP!

"Ow!" cried Hex. He'd landed on something, but it certainly wasn't the ground. He opened his eyes to find himself on the roof of a (fairly battered) police skycar! He'd been caught in mid-air! He peered through the skycar's domed glass roof to see Opo and Dooper.

"Hi Hex!" cried Dooper, waving. "Look what we found!"

"What did – where did – how did –?" began Hex, pressing his suckers to the roof as hard as he could.

"Don't worry, Hex, you're in safe suckers!" said Opo. "I got top marks in hypersaucer training and this is much easier than that! Now, hang on tight – I'm getting you out of here!"

"WAAH! Keep it steady!" gasped Hex, as the skycar weaved between two towers.

"Wherever we're going, we'd better get there quick – I don't know how much longer he can hold on," said Dooper. "Hey, where *are* we going?" he asked.

"Zeeb's Hypersaucer Emporium," Opo replied. "We're getting Hex off Planet X!"

TAKING CONTROL

The skycar weaved between the city's gleaming spires, as Hex clung on to the roof for dear life.

"C-can we find a place to stop? I'm s-slipping!" screamed Hex from the roof, but then he turned around to see the super sentry-bot zooming after them! "Ignore me! Go faster! GO FASTER!"

"Fasten your seatclamp, Dooper – and hang on, Hex!" cried Opo and hit the accelerator as hard as she could. Hex pressed his suckers harder as the skycar dodged and weaved between buildings.

"Come back here! You can't escape! I

command you not to escape!" howled the empress, as the super sentry-bot pursued them through the city, swatting skycars out of the way in mid-air. "Bah! Enough of this chasing nonsense. Super sentry-bot, lock on death rays!"

As Hex clung on, he craned his neck to see the super sentry-bot, which had stopped in mid-air. For a moment, he thought the empress had given up, but then he saw a flash of green energy.

"It's firing! Dive!" he cried, but it was too late.

ZWAAARK!

The blast struck the back of the skycar, disintegrating its main engine! The skycar lurched and spun in mid-air. Hex's suckers slipped and he was flung through the air at a nearby building! He closed his eyes as he saw the wall rushing towards him. . .

THUD!

"Oof!" cried Hex. He got up, made sure he was still in one piece and looked around. His tele-belt had saved him again! He'd teleported into a small, dark space, surrounded by huge banks of machinery and circuits and a thick jungle of wires.

"Klik-POP?" asked Glitch, rolling out of Hex's pocket on to his shoulder.

"I don't know . . . some kind of computing zone, maybe?" replied a confused Hex. "Look at all this tech! Six-way sensor modulizers, triple reinforced X-tanium coupling rods . . . motherboard *and* fatherboard, even built-in Greentooth®! This is cutting edge robotics. What is this place?"

Hex noticed what looked like a rectangular viewscreen. He made his way over to it and looked out. They were still in the middle of New X City. It was then Hex noticed a smoking, battered-looking police skycar, which had landed roughly on top of a tall

tower. Suddenly, everything made sense.

"Klik-POP?" asked Glitch.

"Yeah, I know *exactly* where we are," said Hex. "We're inside the super sentry-bot! The Hex Effect teleported us inside its head! Look, that's the robot's eye-screen! And there's the power cartridge . . . data bubbles . . . control module. . ."

"Chik-POP! POP?" shouted Glitch, excitedly.

"The control module! Glitch, you're right, I can take control from here!" said Hex. He prised a panel off the primary control module. "If I can just disconnect the empress's command feed. . ."

Hex dashed around the super sentry-bot's head, disconnecting wires, bypassing recognition chips, rerouting binary streams. . .

"Hey, my vid-link's going fuzzy!" screamed the empress from her emerald remote command pod, far away in the palace. "What's happening? Super sentry-bot, acknowledge! Super sentry-bot, are you listening to me?"

"It's working! I think . . . just a few more seconds to lock down the transfer. . ." said Hex, hurrying back to the primary control module.

"Who said that? I hear a voice! Who's there?" screeched the empress, her vid-link flickering to nothing. "It's that child, that monstrous child! He's trying to take control! Someone fetch my royal technicians!"

"Ka-chik POP!" said Glitch.

"Nearly – got it!" said Hex, grabbing hold of the primary control module. "Sorry, Empress – I'm pulling the plug on you."

"What? Don't you dare, you little nudlork! This is my robot! Mine!" screeched the empress, helplessly. "Guards! Technicians! Do something! DO SOMETHiiiiiing. . .!"

And with that, the empress was gone and Hex was in command of the most powerful robot ever built.

"Klik ka-chik POP?" asked Glitch.

"Nah, you'll *always* be my number one bot, Glitch. . ." said Hex, staring out of the super sentry-bot's eye. "But I bet you can't do *this*."

Hex squeezed the control module and zoomed through the sky! He laughed as the super sentry-bot spun gracefully around two buildings. It was much more fun than flying a hypersaucer! Then, after a swoop and a dive, he headed straight for Opo and Dooper's crashed skycar.

"The robot's back to boom us!" screamed Dooper, as the super sentry-bot loomed behind them. "Go! Go! Go!"

"I can't!" shouted Opo, hitting the controls. "We've lost our main engine – we're not going anywhere!"

"Well, it was nice knowing you, Opo. Your brother, not so much," said Dooper, as the super sentry-bot reached out its massive pincers. . .

"Don't worry guys, I've got you," said a booming voice over the super sentry-bot's speakers, as it grabbed hold of the car and lifted it into the air. "Just sit back, relax and enjoy the ride."

"What's going on? I thought we were boomed for sure!" bellowed Dooper, as the vid-screen on the super sentry-bot's chest panel flickered to reveal Hex's face.

"Hex! Is that – how did – are you *inside* that thing?" said Opo.

"Cool, isn't it?" chuckled Hex. "We can take on anything with this robot! But without a hyperdriver, it still can't get me off Planet X. You're right, Opo, we have to get to the hypersaucer emporium, and fast."

"You mean, *that* hypersaucer emporium?"

asked Dooper, peering out of the skycar window. There, far below in the city, was Honest Zeeb's.

Hex landed the super sentry-bot outside the emporium. He peered through the window with its massive, single eye, and spotted Honest Zeeb behind his counter.

"Excuse me, please may I borrow a hypersaucer?" he boomed over the speakers.

"WAAAAAAAH!" screamed Honest Zeeb, and hid under his desk!

"This is the coolest thing that's ever happened to anyone," said Dooper. "You have your very own unstoppable robot! You can do anything, and no one can stop you!"

It was at precisely that moment that the sky began to darken. Hex turned on the super sentry-bot's monitors to find an entire fleet of heavily armed, invasion-ready hypersaucers approaching from the horizon.

"Are – are we being invased?" whispered Dooper.

Within seconds, the largest hypersaucer had floated down to the ground in front of them. Its landing ramp slid open, and after a moment, a familiar figure stepped on to the parking lot.

"Hex-37, what on Planet X do you think you're doing?" came the cry.

"*Mum?*"

SUPER SENTRY-BOT
VS MUM

"I *just* got off the holo-vid with Her Majestic Green, the Empress Valoona XIII," said Hex's mum, as she strode towards the giant sentry-bot. "She told me someone took control of her super sentry-bot, and that I should get it back."

"Mum, I—" began Hex, desperately trying to disconnect the vid-screen to hide his face.

"I haven't finished! The empress told me she'd sent her new robot to hunt down an enemy of Planet X . . . a traitor! She told me he'd taken control of her robot, and he must be stopped at all costs! Now, who do I know who's an expert at robotics?"

"Klik-ka-chik-klik. . ." said Glitch, and put his head in his pincers.

"You're inside that thing, aren't you?" asked Hex's mum, firmly.

"N-no?" whimpered Hex, cradling the skycar awkwardly.

"Don't lie to me, young man!" shouted Hex's mum. "You don't think I know my son well enough to know when he's gained control of a giant killer robot?"

"This is worse than being boomed!" whispered Dooper from the skycar. "Hex's mum is really strict. . ."

"Shhh! We'll get told off too!" replied Opo.

"Well, what do you have to say for yourself?" said Hex's mum, sternly.

"Sorry, Mum," mumbled Hex.

"Sorry? SORRY?!" screamed his mum. "You're the world's most wanted criminal! You've broken almost every law we have!

What on Planet X were you thinking?"

"I – I wasn't thinking! I'm sorry, Mum, I'm really sorry! I just – I just didn't want to be a space invader. . ."

"Is this what all of this has been about? Because you don't want to be a space invader?" yelled his mum.

"Well, yeah, that and I had to save Dad," said Hex, quietly.

"Your father? What's he got to do with anything? Your father is lost in space!"

"He's not! He's on Earth! And he wants me to go to Earth, too!" yelled Hex.

"Earth? Planet Earth?!" said Hex's mum. "I've never heard such nonsense in my entire life. Now, come out of that giant killer robot at once!"

"But Mum, I can't! I'm escaping!" cried Hex.

"You're doing no such thing!" growled his mum. "Look around you, Hex –

you're surrounded by an entire fleet of hypersaucers – how on Planet X are you planning to get past them, hmm?"

Hex bowed his head in despair. His mum was right – he'd blown it. He'd been caught, green-suckered, and there was nothing he could do.

Then he remembered he was in control of the most powerful robot on Planet X. Hex put the skycar gently on the ground.

"You should probably find somewhere to hide," said Hex. "This might get a little bit messy."

"Why?" said Opo, as she and Dooper clambered out of the skycar. "What are you going to do?"

"I'm waiting! Are you coming out of there, or not?" asked Hex's mum, sternly.

Hex narrowed his eyes and gripped the primary control module tightly.

"Not a chance," he said, and flew the super

sentry-bot straight at the hypersaucer fleet!

"Hex-37, don't you dare even think about – uh-oh," began Hex's mum. "Evasive manoeuvres!"

The fleet scattered, but the super sentry-bot, under Hex's control, was too fast for them. It headbutted two hypersaucers out of the way, before grabbing another out of the air. The robot held it like a frisbee, and then flung it at another hypersaucer! An almighty **KRuNG!!** filled the air, before both ships spiralled out of control and were sent crashing to the ground.

"I'm taking those hypersaucers out of your pocket money, Hex-37! And – and I'm stopping your pocket money, too!" yelled Hex's mum. "All hypersaucers, regroup! Green formation! Disable that robot, but don't destroy it . . . or I'll disintegrate you all myself!"

"POP! Ka-chik. . ." said Glitch.

"Actually, she's taking it better than I expected," said Hex, as a dozen hypersaucers zoomed towards him, their ray beams streaking forth. Hex activated the super sentry-bot's force field, reflecting the rays back at them! As more hypersaucers fell out off the sky, the bot stopped two mid-flight and held them like a pair of giant cymbals. It began crushing the advancing spaceships between them, or swatting them aside like they were pesky shriek-flies.

"That's it! I'm revoking your holo-vid privileges for a year! No, two! No, for ever!" yelled Hex's mum.

On the ground, Opo and Dooper watched in awe of their new friend, the unstoppable robot, from the cover of the hypersaucer emporium, until a large shadow loomed over them.

"You're not getting away from me this time, you little nudlorks," snarled a voice.

They spun around to find Honest Zeeb, his suckers clenched. "You're going to pay for what you did. I'm going to bash you both into gloop!"

Dooper and Opo looked at each other . . . and then Dooper drew his ray-gun from his tele-belt.

"Stun or mutate?" he asked, his suckers hovering over the dial.

"Oh, mutate, *definitely*," smiled Opo.

"Now, hang on. . ." squeaked Zeeb. "Let's not get carried away, I was only joking! I love kids! Especially ones who try to steal my hypersaucers! Let's work something—"

"BOOM!" shouted Opo, and Dooper instantly fired! The beam hit Zeeb, who immediately sprouted a second head and yellow scales. Seconds later, he shrank down to the size of a magna-boot, grew a dozen new legs and scuttled off in horror!

"Yep, this is definitely better than space invaser training," chuckled Dooper.

Meanwhile, Hex's super sentry-bot had already crushed, crunched or swatted two-thirds of the 101st hypersaucer fleet.

"I'm going to give you such a piece of my mind when I get you home!" shouted Hex's mum. "Enough's enough! You've had your fun, now surrender, we have you surrounded on all sides!"

"Mum's got a point, Glitch," said Hex, checking the anti-matter battery readings as the hypersaucers approached from every angle. "This robot may be unstoppable, but the empress didn't charge it – we're already down to fourteen per cent of our power! We have to finish this, and quickly."

"Klik-ka-chik POP?" asked Glitch.

"Actually, I was sort of hoping you'd think of something," said Hex, chewing nervously on a sucker.

"Ka-chik POP! Chik-ka-klik POP! Ka-chik?" said Glitch.

"Hey, that might just work! Hang on to something. . ." said Hex. As the hypersaucers closed in, Hex began to spin the super sentry-bot in the air! Faster and faster, until it was a blur of green and silver!

"What's he up to now?" said Hex's mum. "Third wave, keep moving! Box him in!"

"H-h-h-hold on, G-Glitch!" said Hex as the robot spun faster and faster. Hex crossed his suckers and then activated the super sentry-bot's shoulder cannons.

ZWAAARK! ZWAARK! ZWAARK! ZWAARK! ZWAARK! ZWAARK! ZWAAAAAARK!

Beams shot out in every direction, filling the sky! As much as the hypersaucers tried to dodge and weave, they couldn't avoid the barrage – every ship in a hundred-metre radius was blasted out of the air! Of the 101st hypersaucer fleet, only his mum's ship, far below on the hypersaucer forecourt, had been spared from destruction.

"We did it . . . we did it!" cried Hex. "And it's a good job too – that last trick cost us the rest of our power. We've got nothing left. . ."

"I am very disappointed in you, Hex-37," said Hex's mum, climbing back into her hypersaucer. She locked on to the super sentry-bot with her ray-cannons. "This is going to hurt me more than it hurts you."

ZWAAAAARK!

ESCAPE FROM PLANET X (2ND ATTEMPT)

Hex's mum fired a single shot from her hypersaucer's ray-cannon. It hit the super sentry-bot with uncanny accuracy, knocking out its anti-gravity generator and guidance systems in one go. Hex and Glitch were thrown off balance as the "unstoppable" robot sank slowly, crashing through the roof of the hypersaucer emporium.

"Glitch! Are you OK? Where are you?" said Hex, scrabbling around in the dark of the super sentry-bot's head.

"Klik-ka-chik! Klik-POP!" replied Glitch, tangled in a mass of loose wires.

"Come on, we have to get out of here, Mum

will be here any minute!" Hex said. "And I think I'd rather be disintegrated than face her after this."

As if on cue, the eye-screen of the super sentry-bot was shattered in a flash of death ray energy! Hex huddled in the darkness, fearing the worst, but when he finally opened his eyes, there was Dooper, blowing the smoke from the end of his ray-gun.

"Come on, Hex! Your mum's just landed and she doesn't look happy!" he said.

"You came back for me!" cried Hex.

"We never left – we were too busy watching you take down the entire hypersaucer fleet!" said Opo, proudly.

"I guess that was pretty cool," said Hex, blushing a deep green. He grabbed Glitch and scrambled out of the giant robot. Hex could already see his mum. She was out of her hypersaucer and striding across the forecourt towards them.

"Hex-37, you get back here right now!" yelled his mother. Hex didn't listen. He and his friends darted into Honest Zeeb's office. Hex slid across the picture of the plump planetexian children, revealing the secret elevation tube. One anti-gravity ride later and Hex, Opo and Dooper were confronted with the sight of the twenty battle-worn hypersaucers.

"So, which one should I take?" asked Hex.

"Whichever one gets us out of here the fastest!" said Opo, grabbing a set of keys from the wall. She waved them around, and with a *bip-bip!* the ramp on the nearest hypersaucer slid open. The three of them stopped, staring at the open door.

"Well, I guess this is it, time to go," said Hex, looking down at his magna-boots. "Look, I, uh, I just want you to know, I really appreciate what you've both done for me, and – wait . . . did you say get 'whichever one gets *us* out'?"

"Well, of course – we're coming with you," said Opo.

"Yeah! We're the secretly-don't-want-to-be-space-invasers!" bellowed Dooper.

"That – that'd be great!" began Hex, but then shook his head. "Wait . . . if you come with me, I don't think you can ever come back. You'll never see anyone on Planet X ever again. And that's if we even make it out of here alive."

Opo and Dooper looked at each other. Then, after a long moment, they both grinned.

"Sounds good to me . . . and anyway, how would you cope without us?" said Opo.

"Team Dooper, Hex and Opo! BOOM!" bellowed Dooper.

"Ka-chik-POP!" huffed Glitch.

"Yeah, and Glitch," laughed Hex. "Sounds like a full hypersaucer crew to me!"

Team Dooper, Hex, Opo and Glitch hurried

inside the hypersaucer. It looked just like the one Hex had piloted during his training, except a lot more dusty. He brushed the dust off the control panel and pressed the big, green START button. He heard the hum of the engines and then de-clamped the moorings and wrapped his suckers around the controls.

"OK – here goes nothing. . ." he said.

"Young man, step away from that control panel this instant!" said a stern voice. Hex spun around to see his mother, standing in the open doorway.

"Mum! I—" began Hex.

"Don't even bother trying to talk your way out of this, Hex. You've had your fun, but this silliness has to stop, right now!"

"It's not silliness!" cried Hex. "I don't want to be a space invader, Mum. I never have."

"Oh, Hex, that's nonsense – everyone

wants to be a space invader," huffed Hex's mum.

"I don't! And neither does Opo, or Dooper, or probably *loads* of planetexians! Why do you think this place even exists? It's because we all want to leave. Everyone's hoping the next Planet X will be better than the last, but it never is! It's just the same . . . and it's never going to stop. Well, I've had enough! Just like Dad had enough. . ."

"Not this again! How many times do I have to tell you, your father is gone for ever, lost in space!" growled Hex's mother.

"But he isn't lost! He's living a new life, a life free of space invading, far away from here! And he's here, on my P.A.D., because he looked for me – because he wants me to join him," said Hex. He held up his P.A.D. and turned it on. "Dad? It's me. I'm with Mum," said Hex.

"He's – he's really there?" said Hex's mum,

suddenly looking a little emotional.

> **HELLO, VEXXA. IT'S ME.**

Hex's Mum took a sharp breath. "Hex-36? Is that really you?"

> **GOOD TO HEAR YOUR VOICE. I HAVEN'T SEEN YOU SINCE THE SOLAR ECLIPSE OF '98.**

"Oh, Hex-36 . . . that was the night you were lost in space," replied Hex's mum, putting a sucker over her circulatory organ.

> **I KNOW. I STILL THINK BACK TO THAT NIGHT. YOU LOOKED A RADIANT SHADE OF GREEN. I BET YOU HAVEN'T CHANGED A BIT.**

"You always were a sweet-talker. . ." said Hex's mum, a tear welling up in her eye. Then, suddenly, she shook her head and gritted her teeth. "Oh, no you don't! Don't think you can charm me, not after all these years – that was always your way out! You being alive doesn't change a thing! Do you realize how much trouble you've caused for Hex-37? What were you thinking, contacting him after all this time?"

I SUPPOSE I WAS THINKING HE MIGHT NOT WANT TO BE A SPACE INVADER.

"And he was right, Mum," interrupted Hex. "I don't. None of us do."

"But don't you see? It's too late! I could usually pull some strings, but not after all this! The empress had already launched another hypersaucer fleet before I blew up the super sentry-bot – there's no way I can stop you from being disintegrated!"

"Yeah, I sort of thought that might be the case . . . sorry about that," said Hex.

"There's nothing I can do. . ." said Hex's mum, suddenly looking a little sad. "Except . . . except let you go."

"What?" asked Hex, Opo, Dooper and Hex's dad together. Even Glitch made a confused pop.

"Hex, I've dedicated my life to space invading. I've put it before my happiness, my marriage, even before you," confessed his mother, sadly. "Well, I may be a merciless conqueror of worlds, but I'm also your mum. I think I can put space invading second – for an hour or so. Now, all I can promise you is a head start – but I'm pretty sure that'll get you safely off Planet X."

"But what about the empress? Won't she want to come after us?" asked Hex.

"Not if she doesn't know you've left. As far as she's concerned, you could all have been disintegrated in the battle with my hypersaucers."

"Are – are you sure? I mean . . . I can go? And you're not disappointed in me?" said Hex. His mother just shook her head and gave him a hug.

"Hex, I think I always knew this would happen. You may not be a born space invader – but you do have a lot of remarkable gifts . . . and you're very good at blowing things up, which has to count for something!" laughed his mum, but after a moment, she began to cry. She wiped a tear away with her sucker, and smiled a wide smile. "Now off you go, Hex, before I change my mind. Oh, and good luck."

And with that, Hex's mum walked down the hypersaucer ramp and waved a sucker as the door closed.

"That was close! I thought we were in so much trouble," said Dooper.

"Me too," said Opo.

ME TOO!

"Klik-POP!" said Glitch.

Hex just smiled, and then secretly wiped

a tear away. He guided the hypersaucer out of the hangar. They zoomed down a long tunnel, finally emerging into the bright morning light. As they sped into the sky, Hex suddenly felt freer than he ever had . . . until he spotted a hundred hypersaucers hot on his tail.

"More of them! Your mum was right – it's a whole other fleet!" cried Opo. "Hex, turn on the hyperdriver, quick! Get us out of here!"

"It's still charging up – this thing hasn't been flown for years! I need ten more seconds!" said Hex.

"They'll have boomed us to pieces by then!" shouted Dooper.

At that very moment, Hex's mum raced into the parking lot. She looked into the sky, to see the hypersaucers race after Hex.

"UNAUTHORIZED LAUNCH IN SECTOR 5788," said the hypersaucer captain.

"LOOKS LIKE AN ESCAPE ATTEMPT. PILOTS, LOCK ON TARGET AND PREPARE TO FIRE!"

"No!" shouted Hex's mum. "Hypersaucer fleet, this is Captain Vexxa! Let that ship go! It's just a decoy, probably piloted by remote control. The criminals have been . . . dealt with."

"ARE YOU SURE?" said the captain. "I'VE BEEN GIVEN STRICT INSTRUCTIONS TO DISINTEGRATE ANYTHING EVEN SLIGHTLY SUSPICIOUS LOOKING. . ."

"I *said* let it go!" growled Hex's mum. "It's all over, Captain. They're gone . . . for ever. Now get back here, that's an *order*."

"UH, YES MA'AM. . ." said the captain. "HYPERSAUCERS, BREAK OFF PURSUIT!"

"They're going away . . . they're leaving!" said Opo, watching the hypersaucers return to the city. "I don't get it. They had us dead in their sights. . ."

"Thanks, Mum," whispered Hex, as the hyperdriver reached full power. Hex pulled the big, green lever and the hypersaucer shot through the atmosphere at faster-than-light speed, disappearing into hyperspace in the blink of an eye.

GREAT HEXPECTATIONS

After an hour or so of zooming through hyperspace, it became clear to Hex, Opo and Dooper that they were not being followed. His mum had kept her promise – they were free. Relieved, they sat back in the hypersaucer as they streaked across an unknown, star-filled wilderness. It stretched out endlessly in every direction, and seemed to all three of them to be a universe of possibilities.

"I like it out here. Everything's . . . less green," said a wide-eyed Dooper.

"Yeah . . . and Earth's out there somewhere. All we have to do is find it," said Hex, and then looked down at his P.A.D. "We're on our way, Dad! The only thing is . . . how do we get to Earth?"

EASY! I'M PATCHING IN THE CO-ORDINATES NOW, HEX. BASICALLY, JUST TAKE A LEFT AT THE ASTEROID BELT, RIGHT AT THE BIG STAR CLUSTER, AND THEN HEAD STRAIGHT FOR THE ENORMOUS, SCARY-LOOKING BLACK HOLE. . .

"Really? I mean, you're sure we're going to be OK?" asked Hex, turning left at the asteroid belt. "What if the whole flying into a black hole thing doesn't work the same way for us as it did for you?"

WHAT DO YOU MEAN?

"Klik-kik-ka-chik POP!" said Glitch.

"Exactly! What if, instead of being transported safely through the black hole and appearing somewhere sort of near Planet

Earth, we just get lost for ever, or crushed to bits by massive gravitational forces?"

"Nobody said anything about losing or crushing!" said Dooper, nervously. "I'd rather be a space invaser than get lost and crushed!"

"Oh come on, Dooper – it's not like we ever really thought Hex knew what he was doing. . ." answered Opo.

"I'll take that as a compliment," said Hex with a shrug, veering right at the giant star cluster.

DON'T WORRY, EVERYONE. THE HEX EFFECT WILL GET YOU THROUGH, MARK MY WORDS. I'LL SEE YOU ON THE OTHER SIDE – ON EARTH! YOU'LL LOVE IT – I'LL PUT THE KETTLE ON, AND WE CAN ALL HAVE TEA AND BISCUITS WHEN YOU ARRIVE.

"Tee ant biskips? What's that?" asked Dooper.

IT'S LIKE GLOOP, EXCEPT COMPLETELY DIFFERENT! PLUS, IT ACTUALLY TASTES OF SOMETHING. YOU'LL LOVE IT!

"Better than Gloop?" bellowed Dooper. "No way!"

HEH . . . I THINK YOU'RE ALL GOING TO LIKE IT HERE. EARTHLINGS ARE GREAT – IF A LITTLE BIT WEIRD. AND DO YOU KNOW WHAT THE BEST THING IS? IF YOU TELL AN EARTHLING THAT YOU'RE AN ALIEN FROM ANOTHER PLANET, THEY DON'T EVEN BELIEVE YOU! THEY DON'T EVEN THINK ALIENS EXIST . . . WELL, MOST OF THEM.

"They sound a bit stupid," said Dooper, accidentally poking himself in the eye.

I'LL SEE YOU AND YOUR FRIENDS VERY SOON, SON. TRUST IN THE HEX EFFECT – IT'LL BRING YOU HERE SAFE AND SOUND, AND I'LL BE WAITING.

"Yeah, trust in the Hex Effect!" said Hex,

almost believing it. As they peered at the viewscreen, the black hole loomed large before them. Hex guided the hypersaucer straight for it. "Hang on to your antennae, everyone – here we go!"

"Uh, Hex, you *do* know what you're doing, right?" whispered Opo, suddenly a little nervous.

"Of course! Don't worry – I have a feeling our luck is looking up!" said Hex. A moment later, the hypersaucer immediately began to rattle and shake, and the onboard computer immediately started shouting very loudly.

"ALERT! YOU ARE APPROACHING A BLACK HOLE! THIS IS A VERY BAD IDEA! PULL UP! CERTAIN DEATH INEVITABLE!"

"Or maybe not. . .!" muttered Hex. The hypersaucer felt as if it was about to fall apart! Hex, Opo, Dooper and Glitch grabbed on to whatever they could find, and prepared themselves for the worst as the hypersaucer was pulled towards the black hole.

"S-s-s-sorry I d-dragged you into th-this!" cried Hex, suddenly feeling less confident about his dad's plan as he felt his teeth shake in his head.

"N-n-no p-p-problem!" replied Opo. "Th-th-that's what f-f-f-friends are f-f-for!"

"T-t-team D-d-d-ooper, H-h-h-h-Hex and O-o-o-. . . oh, well you get the idea!" bellowed Dooper.

"K-k-k-klik-POP!" added Glitch.

By now, the black hole had engulfed them. The three planetexians (and one little robot) closed their eyes tightly as the hypersaucer disappeared into the void. The noise became deafening, as rivets and bolts popped out of the walls, and the whole saucer seemed to be crying out under the strain. Then, suddenly, there was silence. It was quieter than Hex had ever known.

Hex opened his eyes and tried to look out

of the viewscreen, but it quickly became so bright that he had to look away, as if everywhere was filling up with stars. Hex closed his eyes again, as everything turned white. Then:

"ALERT! IMPACT IN 30 SECONDS! PULL UP! CERTAIN DEATH INEVITABLE – I MEAN IT THIS TIME!"

"What the – what's going on?" said Hex. A planet appeared in the viewscreen, and they were heading straight for it! Hex tried to pull the hypersaucer up for a proper landing, but it was too late.

"WHAT DID I TELL YOU? CERTAIN DEATH INEVITABLE!" screamed the onboard computer.

"That's really not helping! Hang on, everyone!" he cried, as the hypersaucer ploughed into the planet's surface! It skidded and bounced along the ground, driving through mounds of grey dust, before finally coming to a bumpy halt.

"We made it . . . we made it! Everyone OK?" asked Hex, counting his suckers.

"BOOM!" shouted Dooper. "That was cool!"

"We're in one piece . . . I can't believe it!" replied a shaken Opo.

"Klik-POP! Ka-chik!" said Glitch.

"Yeah, Glitch is right, we're only *just* in one piece," said Hex. "Looks like the hyperdriver's OK, but it's going to take a few hours to repair the guidance system. But we made it . . . we actually made it!" he cried, grabbing his P.A.D. "Dad, are you there? It worked! We're on Planet Earth!"

> HEX! GREAT TO HEAR FROM YOU, SON! IS EVERYONE OK?
> WHERE ARE YOU? SEND ME YOUR COORDINATES.
> DID ANYONE SEE YOU LAND?

"Coordinates . . . 4581.09," said Hex,

checking the controls, and then he peered out of the viewscreen at an endless, grey desert. "There doesn't seem to be anyone around. Actually, there doesn't seem to be much of anything. It doesn't look quite like I imagined. It's just dust."

BUT THOSE COORDINATES DON'T . . . WAIT. LOOK UP, HEX, INTO THE SKY. WHAT DO YOU SEE?

"Nothing, just space," said Hex, staring up. "Outer space, and stars, just the normal stuff. Oh, and a big blue planet in the distance."

DID YOU SAY BIG . . . BLUE PLANET? I DON'T KNOW HOW TO TELL YOU THIS, SON, BUT I'M AFRAID THAT BIG BLUE PLANET IS EARTH! YOU'RE ON THE MOON . . . A FEW HUNDRED THOUSAND MILES OFF TARGET.

"A few hundred thousand miles? Just my luck! Stupid Hex Effect! What do we do now? The hyperdriver's wrecked!" growled Hex.

"Does that mean we have to live here, now?" said Dooper, sadly. "I was looking forward to tee ant biskips. . ."

> DON'T PANIC, SON, YOU'RE GOING TO BE FINE.
> AND YOU'RE NEARLY HOME. . .

Hex clenched his suckers and took a deep gill-breath.

"Dad's right, we'll get there – I promise. We didn't come this far to give up now," said Hex, inspecting the hypersaucer controls.

He started rushing around the hypersaucer, making adjustments. "I'm pretty sure we can take off using the thrusters. I just need to recalibrate the navi-module . . . divert power to the anti-matter chamber . . . reset launch coding . . . there!"

Hex's sucker hovered over the big, green button. He stared out of the viewscreen again at the planet in the distance. Earth looked so close that he could reach out and touch it. What's more, it looked like *home*.

"Put the kettle on, Dad, we'll see you in a few days. . ." said Hex, and pressed the button. The hypersaucer chugged and groaned, and began to shake so hard it felt as if it was coming apart!

". . . With any luck!" added Hex – and crossed his suckers.

Guy Bass grew up dreaming of being a superhero – he even had a Spider-Man costume. The costume doesn't fit any more, so Guy now contents himself with writing books and plays. His current books include the *Gormy Ruckles* series, *Alien Invasion* and *Alien Escape*, and *Dinkin Dings* (winner of the 2010 Blue Peter Book Award Most Fun Book With Pictures). Guy lives in London with his wife and no dog, yet.

Find out more at
www.guybass.com